In loving memory of my dear parents.

This book stands as a testament to the boundless support and encouragement you provided throughout my life's journey. Your presence is felt on every page.

MICHAEL J. KUNDU

THE LONELY PRISONER

MINDSTIR MEDIA

Published by MindStir Media, LLC
45 Lafayette Rd | Suite 181| North Hampton, NH 03862 | USA
1.800.767.0531 | www.mindstirmedia.com

Printed in the United States of America.
ISBN-13: 978-1-962987-38-7

*This is more than just a crime mystery story.
It is also about life and how we live it today.*

Contents

Chapter 1: The Cell 1

Chapter 2: The Guard 10

Chapter 3: A Game of Chess 19

Chapter 4: The Meaning of Life 27

Chapter 5: The Years Pass By 32

Chapter 6: Outside 40

Chapter 7: Home 47

Chapter 8: The Crime Scene 53

Chapter 9: The Witness 65

Chapter 10: Eileen 73

Chapter 11: Vincent 82

Chapter 12: The Park 88

Chapter 13: Judge Carter 94

Chapter 14: Brian 101

Chapter 15: The Cemetery 109

Chapter 16: Tom Bane 119

Chapter 17: The Library 130

Chapter 18: The Accusation 140

Chapter 19: The Girl 147

Chapter 20: The Puzzle 153

Chapter 21: The Mayor 160

Chapter 22: Jack 167

Chapter 23: Cat Out of the Bag 175

Chapter 24: Contrition 182

Reflection from the Author 188

CHAPTER 1

The Cell

"One-two-three wall. One-two-three door, one-two-three wall."

Michael Fletcher counted his steps slowly in his new stay, the place where he just entered and where he would spend his next twenty-six years. The echo of the heavy steel door, closing behind him, still rang in his ears. He turned and sat on his new bed, which ran along the side wall, fixed securely to the ground. He looked up and stared at a stainless-steel toilet and a sink just in front of him. A toothbrush and toothpaste were provided. The walls were bare and white, with one single empty shelf on the opposite side. The floor was a hard, dark single surface, the ceiling was low, and the room smelled of disinfectant. Michael just sat there, stunned, both hands grasping his knees.

He was only twenty-five years old when he was found guilty. Tall, clever, friendly and handsome with his dark-brown hair and matching eyes, he had all the traits for a successful life. However, now it had abruptly ended. He sat there, still staring at the pale wall in this small prison cell, for something he had not understood and would never come to terms with. He was now locked away in a tiny corner of the world. It was like a bad dream from which he hoped to be awakened at any moment.

He looked down at his only possession that remained: his white sneakers. An orange jumpsuit and a pair of dark socks were given to him; all the rest he was asked to put in a cardboard box when he entered prison, one

1

arm attached to a bulky police officer by a pair of handcuffs. The box was labelled with his name and birth date, then taken away for storage.

He had to strip down, naked, and endured an uncomfortable procedure that seemed to last forever to ensure he had nothing unwanted with him. He felt like a member of a lost cattle herd, driven, beaten from one room to the other, just enduring time.

He was then handed his new clothes and asked to dress under supervision. He was escorted through endless corridors, separated by sliding barred gates, when finally, he arrived in an open space with gangways passing on several levels, lit by bright fluorescent lighting along its ceilings. He was guided past countless doors, plain, fully sealed, green-painted. He could not see who was behind any of them, but he guessed other prisoners. Now he was one of them. At one moment he was instructed to stop walking while one guard took out a set of keys, opening his new stay.

Reality brought him back to his cage, sitting on a springy bed. The mattress was foam, wrapped by a clean, grey sheet. At one end were two brown blankets and on top of it a cushion, covered by a matching grey pillow cover. He was alone, locked away and felt betrayed by the world. *So, what shall I do now?* Michael thought, looking around, his hands grasping his knees even tighter. Blurred images, the torment of his trial and the mysterious night that all led to his arrest, were flashing in his head.

When Judge Carter slammed down the hammer, condemning him to spending the best years of his life behind bars, little explanation was given, even though the proceedings seemed to last an eternity. Michael remembered that there was a witness who saw him at the scene of the crime, but little remained in his recollection of what had possibly happened.

He vaguely recalled that he returned quite drunk after a good time at a bar with some friends. It was a chilly night in February 1996. He folded up the collar of his coat, tucked his hands deep into the pockets, and started walking down the doomy lanes of the older part of the city in the early morning, towards his newly rented flat. The streets were deserted, minus the odd homeless folk sleeping on the ground, wrapped in blankets on the warmth of the occasional ventilation hole.

His footsteps were echoing in the alleys, and then suddenly all went incredibly fast. The body, the weapon, the flashing blue lights. And, before he knew what had really happened, he found himself in the rear of a police car, his hands tied painfully behind his back with a plastic tie-down cutting into his wrist. He was taken to the local police station and into a small bright room by the officers, where they questioned him about his whereabouts during the evening and what he did after he left the bar. Michael was tired and kept repeating that he did not remember much. His rights may have been read to him; his recollections were vague, and the questioning continued almost till dawn. He woke up on a hard bench in a small single cell and was then given a black coffee. The occurrences of the previous night were fazed. Neither did he recall that he signed his name onto some papers that were put in front of him. The real implication of this was only revealed by Vincent Graham.

Vincent was a young, local lawyer working for the city. He held a black leather binder in his left hand, while offering his right promptly to Michael, as he walked into his cell. He was a bit shorter than Michael and slim, probably in his late twenties or early thirties and debonair. He was smartly dressed in a dark linen suit, white shirt, and a red tie. His hair was pitch black and nicely slicked back. After the first introduction, he explained that he took his case pro bono. Michael knew the meaning well. He was a graduate, not in law, but understood that there was no charge for representing him.

Vincent had asked to speak to him alone, so they were taken to a small bare room. The lawyer took a seat directly across a square table and opened a leather binder, which revealed a cream legal pad with a pen stuck across the top. A flickering neon strip on the ceiling emitted a buzzing sound, which made Michael dizzy, and the exposure to the harsh light put a strain on his sagging eyes. He had had a rough night in custody, had barely gotten any sleep and his brain struggled to function.

Vincent took his pen, clicked it, and smiled weakly. "Okay Michael, I am here to represent you, and everything we discuss will remain between us and in this room." He paused and looked at his client intensely. "So, do tell me Michael," Vincent said in a smooth tone, leaning forward, "what happened last night?"

Michael was not quite sure how to answer, as he still did not recall what had really occurred. "Hmm, why am I actually here?"

"You do not remember anything from last night?"

"Not a great deal, honestly. I left the bar and now I am here. I've had a very tiresome night, haven't slept, I have a throbbing behind my eyes and my brain is switched off. So please believe me, somehow my memory is very foggy."

"Okay, let us start with the basics. I am here to help you, to defend you. You are a suspect in a crime that was committed last night. Are you sure you do not recall anything?"

Michael placed his elbows on the table and leaned his head on his fore-fingers, massaging his temples slowly. He looked up, took a deep breath, and then glanced at his lawyer.

"Well, as I just said, I was at a bar, had some drinks, then left on my own and wanted to walk home. Then, suddenly there was a body on the ground … yeah, I sort of remember that. He was not lying there like all the other homeless on one side of the pathway, well tucked away on their cardboard. He was in the middle of the pavement … that was strange. I remember kneeling down and seeing this person still moving, but there was something sticking out of his body. He had his back turned towards me. I really do not remember, but I must have touched or grabbed it when I turned him on his back. It was dark, and this person was groaning. I was not really myself, as I had quite a bit to drink. My actions were not exactly controlled."

"And then?"

"Well, nothing really, I do not know what to say, I don't remember much more, apart from the flashing blue lights that arrived shortly after. Hmm, what happened to this guy and where is he?"

The attorney scribbled something down, looked up, held the pen firmly in his hand, and spoke. "Okay, let us start from the beginning. Which bar did you go to? And who was with you?"

Michael answered all his questions, starting from meeting up for a get together with some colleagues from work. They were new friends really. Michael had been in town only a few weeks since graduating in economics. He worked as an accountant in a local tax office. It was Friday night and after some fast food at the corner of a street they headed for some drinks at a bar called The Duke. It was the usual chit-chat, girls, sports and before he realized it, it was about one in the morning. He left alone. Yes, his new friends wanted to shoot some pool in an adjacent room, but he decided to leave. He was tired and was due to take the train in the early morning to see his parents for the weekend. He was on his own as he left and walked home.

"One moment, let me stop you there. You left this bar called The Duke on your own, right? And it was about one in the morning?"

Michael nodded.

"How do you know? Did you check your watch?"

"I do not wear one, there was a clock on the wall. I asked David—he was one of the guys I was with—how long they usually stayed. David told me that it depends. Most Friday nights they remained until four in the morning. In a back room, you were able to play pool for money after a certain hour. I did not really fancy this idea, as I don't know how to play anyway, and I am sort of short on cash, as I just upfronted a three-month lease for my flat. So, I looked at the clock on the wall, noticed it was one in the morning, and left."

Seemingly professional and detailed, the attorney jotted all of this information down while giving the occasional nod. Michael watched him as he tried to recollect the fuzzy events of the previous night, but he still had difficulties. His tiredness overcame him, and he was struggling to stay awake.

"To get this down for my notes, your friend's name was David. Got a full name and address? Also, what are the names of the other friends? Best to write their full names and position at work down here."

Vincent pushed across a loose piece of paper and another pen that he took from the inside pocket of his suit. Vincent wanted to get their names right and asking for the exact spelling would be futile, in view of his client's state, so it was better he wrote them down himself.

"I assume they were all guys from your workplace?"

"Yes, they were."

"It's best to also give me their telephone number so I can reach them. I of course need to check up with them to verify the time. Their office number will be fine. I assume they have the same number as you, just the extension is different. In case you do not know their number, don't worry. While you are at it, please also note down the exact address of the tax office where you are employed and the name of the department manager or your boss, there. There are likely different office locations in town."

Michael sighed and wrote everything neatly onto the sheet, while Vincent watched him pensively. His head was hurting, but he put in his best effort.

"Thank you, Michael. I know it's hard to do this early in the morning, but we must get the details matched up. So, try to collect and start again with what happened next, after you left the bar."

Michael leaned back. "Eh, well, I just remember walking home and seeing this guy lying in the street, as I already told you."

"Let me ask, do you remember how long you were walking until you saw the body?"

"Pfff, I have no clue, the bar is not that far from where I live, maybe 15 minutes from my flat, I guess I was about halfway."

"Fine, let us start there, when you found the body. Try to recall all you can. Please try to be precise, this is extremely important. I need to know the full details."

"Well, as I said, I was walking, and I saw somebody lying there."

"Are you sure he was lying there when you saw him? He was not walking towards you or in any other direction?"

"No, no, he was really sprawled on his side on the ground, I am sure, man."

"What did he look like?"

"The street was very poorly lit, it was dark as I just told you, so I did not see much. His back was facing me. I noticed him moving and groaning, and I bent down and touched him."

Vincent put down his pen again and asked, "What do you mean by *you touched him?*"

"Look, I do not know how often I need to repeat this. I cannot recall very much. I turned him around, that is all. Really, I had a bit too much to drink. So, tell me, what actually happened to this guy, is he okay?"

"How much did you have to drink?"

"Probably six to eight beers, but I did not have much for dinner. The deli at the corner we were at before wasn't great."

"You're sure, just the beers?"

"Yes, I think so, nothing else, just beer."

Vincent nodded while continuing to write everything down on his legal pad, then put down his pen again and looked straight at his client.

"Look Michael, right now all I can tell you about this guy, I do not know his name yet, or who he is, but to put it simply, he is dead. He was found by the police upon arrival, and you were at the scene. He was stabbed by a large knife; your prints are on the weapon. I am not implying anything here, but as your attorney, you must help me to better understand what happened. He did have a substantial amount of money on him, and it was literally falling out of his pockets."

Michael swallowed hard, blinked, and looked at his blue fingers. During the night, a deputy took his prints. He had to place all ten fingertips on an ink pad and then, one by one, the officer placed each finger on a sheet of paper, identifying each one separately, meticulously. She started with the thumb on the left hand and finished with his pinky on the right hand. After that, mugshots were taken from all sorts of angles. It was just like in the movies, with a board behind him with measurements, showing his height.

He buried his head into his hands, scratched his hair and looked up. "Look, I do not know what you are trying to say, but I had nothing to do with this—I just found him. Was there nobody else who saw what happened?"

"We will of course look into this, and the police are issuing a full report of their findings. But right now, there seems to have been nobody else other than you on the scene. At least, so far nobody has come forward, except of course the person who phoned the police. He saw you leaning over the body. These things may take time, as they are searching for further witnesses. A question, Michael, how much do you earn? I understand that you paid in advance for three months of your rent, and you mentioned that you were short on cash." Vincent quickly jotted a few words on his pad.

"This is ridiculous. Just because I am short of cash, I am not going to attack or kill someone for some handful of money! This is completely off the scene. I—I, do not know what more to say. You must believe me; I am telling you I had nothing to do with this!" Michael was now awake, he was slowly understanding the seriousness of the situation, but was feeling weak and helpless.

"Okay, don't worry. Details of your account may have to be disclosed though, should it become a proceeding in court. Have you been given the opportunity to phone a family member? You have the right to do so."

Michael nodded. "I prefer not to. I do not want anybody to worry, for the moment." He recalled that he was due to visit his parents today, but let it pass. It was not the first time that he'd skipped the visit. New life in a foreign city had its attractions that a known place from birth did not.

Vincent looked at his client sincerely but also in a tedious manner. Pro bono was sometimes not all that enticing, but essential in his profession to ascend to higher levels. Attorneys often showed with eagerness their vast and benevolent experiences, and also engaged in pro bono to fulfill their moral responsibility. What was, of course, most important was to be able to receive higher callings with lucrative salaries. Billing by the hour is what mattered to make a good living. Most lawyers, though, believe in their profession and are honest, and Michael hoped that Vincent was one of them.

"Let us then wrap it up here for the moment, Michael. To take this case further, I will have to do some paperwork."

Vincent pushed across another piece of paper and a business card that he took out of his upper pocket. He placed both in front of his new client and turned them around so that he was able to read them.

"Here, you may now sign. Let me explain this to you. This is an agreement for legal representation. You are therefore accepting that I officially function as your attorney. This means that I can speak for you and give you legal counselling. In other words, I will try my best to help you in your current situation. How does that sound?"

Michael nodded without looking up, reading the one-sided script which was placed in front of him.

"The next thing I will do is question your friends, as they were the last to speak to you prior to the incident. Also, I will have to talk to your employer. They may want to know why you are not turning up to work next week. It means that if all goes well, and you are declared innocent, no matter how long the process, your workplace is secured. If you do not turn up and they do not hear from you, as you understand, they will ask questions and you could lose your job. So, I will therefore take care to explain the situation to them. I assume you are also okay with this?"

Michael nodded once more; his vision was far beyond the script of the paper. Vincent wondered if he was still listening. *Poor boy, rough night, rough morning. Let us see how this turns out ... okay, I've got to get home myself, really.*

"Listen, the police are intending to search your home, where you are staying, to check for possible evidence relating you to the victim. I am entitled to be present during this search. This can, of course, be greatly beneficial for you; I assume that you want me to be there. Once I am through with the initial proceedings, I will come and see you again. This is my card. You are entitled to keep this and you are allowed to call me, but just for any questions and concerns regarding this case. I strongly recommend that you not speak to anybody, as of now. Should somebody want to question you without my presence, it is illegal, if you understand what I mean. My number is on the bottom. Should I not be in my office, you will get my answering machine. Do not by any means say more than your name and that you called. I will get back to you. Any questions?"

Michael slowly shook his head, picked up the pen with his right hand and signed the paper. Then he grasped the business card of Vincent with both hands and transfixed it.

"I can call this number, here, yeah?"

"That's right. Only this number. I cannot promise you that I will come tomorrow, as I have other engagements. It is Sunday anyway. I will check on you on Monday. You will now be taken into custody where you will have to remain until the first hearing in front of a judge. You may be able to get out on bail, should you or a family member be able to fund this, until the official trial and court ruling. However, in view of the current circumstances, I see little chance that this may happen."

Michael shuddered, and suddenly he was back again in this tiny room, his prison cell, breathing heavily. His mind kept wandering between the present and the past. The images and conversations whirled in his head. Police officers, the interrogation, Vincent and then the questionings that were set in motion during the trial. *What went wrong and what could have been done differently?* That is the sequence of questions that mostly came to his mind now. *What went wrong?* he kept on repeating to himself. He was in shock, despondent, and felt like crying. However, the deep and inner sadness hit him so hard, like boulder of stones lying on his chest, that he just sat there paralyzed. He felt empty and isolated from the world, sad and withdrawn. Life seemed to slow down, as a sense of worthlessness overcame him. Any hope that had arisen during the last week for an end to the ordeal had dissipated. He closed his eyes and drifted off again, then opened them once more, hoping to wake up from a nightmare. It was not to be.

CHAPTER 2

The Guard

It was almost dark when Michael heard a flap at the bottom of his cell door open. It flipped upwards towards the outside as he saw a metal tray being pushed through the bottom. Then the flap closed, and a bolt slid across. The cell was completely silent again. On the tray he recognized two slices of brown bread, a few cuts of sausage, a tomato, and an empty plastic glass. When he first entered today, he was told that he could consume the water from his sink. The knot that had formed in his stomach, however, gave him no desire to eat or drink. Instead, he just sat there and looked vacantly at the wall; too great was his state of desperation and the feeling of helplessness that engulfed his body.

The last rays of the sunlight shone through the barred window above him, situated directly opposite the cell door. It was above head-height, so he would have to stand on his bed to look out. So far, he had not moved from the sitting position that he took from the very first moment of entering his cage. It must have been six or seven in the evening, he guessed. They mentioned the words *solitary confinement*, alone in a cell for some time, initially at least, until further notice. He would have no contact with the outside world. He had read many books about crimes and prison sentences; now he was part of these stories. Pushed into another world, forgotten by the rest to rot away in a small room, with little to do. They would allow him to go outside for three hours a day, should his behavior allow it. Additionally, a few chores could be earned to gain some extra cash. The warden, who introduced himself as *The Law*, slowly and meticulously explained the daily routine to his new arrival. His expression was very stern, and he meant every word he said. This Michael immediately understood by the way the warden was talking to him; he probably made the rules and everyone had to obey. He was frightened and had no intention of doing otherwise.

Michael stood up slowly, but instead of taking his tray he climbed onto the bed and stood upright. He was 1.84 meters tall and of medium build. Standing on his toes, he leaned on the window opening that ran slanting, slightly upwards, towards the outside. He glimpsed out beyond the four bars, which ran vertically. All he saw was another cemented wall with dark barbed wire running densely across the top. *Probably the outside prison perimeter*, he thought to himself.

He kept peering out and was lost again in his bitter memories. Vincent Graham, his lawyer, had visited him again the following Monday, after he was arrested the first time. It was late afternoon, almost evening. Vincent disclosed that he entered his flat with the police, who searched the entire place for any evidence or motive connecting him to the deceased. Then they sealed the door.

"Your flat cannot be entered by anybody, not even your relatives, at the moment. You will be able to return, of course, if you are set free. Should you instead be found guilty and sentenced to time in prison, your flat must be emptied by either a family member or it can be arranged by the police. Your belongings will then be stored away. Smaller items can be sent to prison. When your possessions are gone, the owner of the flat will be entitled to dispose of it as he wants. Of course, you will also need to notify your insurance company of your incarceration."

"So, what is going to happen next?" Michael asked in a quivering voice.

"Right now, potential witnesses are being searched and then questioned. All evidence is still being collected. This may take a few days, and then a full report will be filed by the police. There will be a first hearing in front of a judge, probably by the end of this week. The judge will then decide whether there will be a case set against you. As I already explained to you on Saturday, you may be released on bail, or you must remain in custody until the trial. The trial itself may take place very quickly, depending on the agenda of the judge."

"How long would the trial take?"

"It can be over within three to five days. The prosecution and I will have to agree on an impartial jury and the trial will start shortly after. The actual duration of the trial depends often on the length of the questioning of all witnesses and expert-witnesses that the prosecution or the defense will bring as evidence."

Michael nodded and was certainly more awake than last time. "What is an *expert-witness?*"

"Good question, Michael. In simple terms, expert witnesses have specialized skills and knowledge, or experience. They are hired experts in specific fields that make an evaluation and then present their professional opinion on the matter to the court. Let us take the case of the knife that was used in the killing of the victim. You said that you 'just touched it.' The question here is, why were only *your* prints found on the knife. I have this morning checked with an expert on this matter to verify whether it is possible that the real killer may have wiped away his prints or used gloves, and you then only touched or grabbed the weapon accidentally. The expert we are hiring is someone who is going to work for your case; not against it. Still, he needs to testify under oath and should remain unbiased. The prosecution will of course argue to contradict this theory by introducing an expert witness that sees it differently."

"So, the one who is more convincing tends to be believed?"

"Well, most of the time the arguments do bear a great weight. But the finding of a witness that saw you arriving *after* the victim was on the ground is currently my biggest priority. So far, we only have one witness who saw you together with the body; this person also called the police. Little time must have passed between the moment that the victim was stabbed and the moment you arrived. These are crucial seconds where we have no testimonies. After all the cross-examinations of witnesses and expert witnesses, the conclusion of the trial will be a final statement by the prosecution and me to convince the jury one way or the other. Really, at the end you will then be judged guilty or not."

Looking back to the start of the trial, all had seemed to go so well. The court room was packed, all seats were taken and the interest in the case was high as the victim was well known. Michael learned that his name was Flynn Meier. The first order of business was to allow the attorneys to make the opening statement. Both the prosecution and the defense addressed the jury to present their case. Vincent's opening was short but to the point. He clearly explained that his client was only walking home. He did not even know the victim and happened to be at the wrong place at the wrong time. Michael graduated and worked in a secure position for the state, so there was no motive whatsoever to commit a crime. However, as prospective as it all began, the pendulum quickly swung the other way.

Flynn Meier was somebody Michael really did not know at all—neither was he aware that he was the owner of the local casino. Why Flynn had so much cash on him, in the early hours, was not questioned. But it was assumed that Michael Fletcher knew him and that he had the intention of getting the money. Michael was a light gambler and had won often and lost sometimes. His favorite was blackjack. Statistically, of all the casino games you play, playing blackjack gives you the biggest chance of winning. Being an economist and understanding numbers, he mastered that. He had maybe gone to the casino six or seven times since he moved to this city, but not more. It gave him pleasure to sit at the table and play. He had an excellent memory and was able to count cards, giving him a small edge. It was not illegal to do so but was frowned upon by the casinos, and got you thrown out if you were discovered. So, Michael decided not to go often. However, the fact remained that the accused went there, and that meant he must have known the owner, Flynn Meier. Michael was asked by the astute prosecutor if he had been to the casino. He could not deny the fact, as likely there would still be security camera recordings in the archives. Flynn actually, for fun and customer relationship, sometimes functioned as a croupier at the table, dealing the cards for the house. No witness could really recall that Flynn was dealing those very nights when Michael had been to the casino. But due to the fact that the accused was a regular player in the eyes of the prosecution and the fact that Flynn also dealt, a connection was quickly made.

Before Michael knew it, two days had passed. The trial did not last long. The final verdict was that he was guilty of murder. The Honorable Judge Carter was in his late forties and known to be fair and unbiased; however, Michael could not let go of this feeling that he was being despised upon from the very first minute his Honor saw him. Carter was unsmiling and ruthless, almost ferocious during the whole proceeding. The ruling and sentencing were announced like bullets, firing into his chest. No sympathy was shown. Judge Carter repeated his guilt and his duty as judge to condemn him for his committed crime. He did not call it premeditated murder, but second-degree murder, an action during which he stabbed to steal money.

He may not have intended to kill, but he was aware of inflicting great bodily harm, acting with reckless disregard for human life.

Suddenly, Michael heard an observation window slide open on the upper part of his cell door. The sound brought him back to the present and the bed he still stood on, looking out of his window. He turned around and saw through the square opening a set of marine blue eyes peering through the gap on the upper center of the prison door. He did not see more than this. Just a set of friendly looking blue eyes.

"Not hungry?" a voice said, markedly.

"Not really," Michael responded. He assumed it must be a guard, checking upon him. Was it impolite not to eat what he was given? He did not want to cause trouble, so he stepped off his bed, went to the door, bent down, and took the tray. He turned, went to his bed, and sat down, placing the tray on his lap. The pair of eyes kept watching him closely.

"I am Jack, the guard. I am here in the evenings and stay for the night watch."

Michael nodded while he took the bread and the sausage. He put them together and took a full bite. While he chewed slowly, he turned his head and noticed that Jack was watching him intensely. Was he supposed to say something or was it prohibited to speak to the guard? He was unsure how to behave. Surprisingly, the bread was soft, and the sausage was very tasty, though he had no appetite at all. A long and heavy silence reigned, as he also nibbled at the tomato.

"Best to eat up everything you get here; you will need all your strength to make it through."

"Yes sir," Michael mumbled after he quickly swallowed his next bite.

"You can call me Jack, at these hours. There is only me at this time of day, or night if you want to call it this way. But when you are out of your cell, you better stick to *sir*."

"Yes, sir, thank you Jack."

The guard kept watching him through the observation window as he munched away.

"I was told you came only today. It is twenty-six years; I saw it in your file."

Michael took another bite and almost choked when he heard the length of the duration he was supposed to be here.

"It's a long time I suppose, for something you claim not to have done."

Michael looked up at him, surprisingly. "Is that also written in the papers?" He hoped not to come across as contentious, but this comment intrigued him.

"Not directly. I followed your case and most of it is public anyway. The reason for knowing a bit more is that I was a police officer at the crime scene, the day after it happened. I had to go with the second forensic team, during daylight. I was transferred here to this prison unit only a couple of days ago and now I work here as a night-watch."

Michael nodded, put the tray aside on his bed and stood up, taking the plastic cup. He dragged himself to the sink and opened the tap. He put one finger under the water to take a feel of the temperature. He let it run for a few seconds until he felt the stream of water cooling down and then put the cup under it. When almost full, he closed the tap and took a sip. He was thirsty, as he hadn't drunk anything since this morning. It tasted good as he felt the icy water run down his throat. So, he filled another glass and took it back to his tray. He sat back down, picked up the tray again, put it on his lap, and continued eating, slowly. Michael was kept in another prison during the days of the trial and was transferred to this penitentiary only today. Lukewarm, bottled water was all he got during that period. So, he was glad to drink something cooler for once.

"The water is good here; you are lucky. It comes from the local mountain reservoir. It won't give you any problems. It will keep you healthy, as it is of best quality."

"Okay, Jack, good to know. What do I have to do when I have finished eating?"

"Just put everything back on the tray and place it in front of the flap at the bottom of the door. Make sure you always put the plate and the cutlery you were given back. It will be controlled. The cup you may keep."

"Yes, Jack, I have understood."

"You know, you are quite lucky to have landed here. This is a brand-new place, very recently built. You may even be the first one who has entered this cell. The water systems are brand new, therefore also the superior quality of water. The whole complex is very modern and of the most recent technologies, to ensure all goes well."

"Okay, Jack."

"Just stick to the rules and follow the routines. Best to not cause any trouble, then you will be fine."

"It will be some time before I am let outside with the other inmates, I was told. It will depend on my behavior."

"That's right, Michael. Just remain polite, do as you're told, then you will be okay. The warden keeps books on everyone and makes the rules. He will decide what will happen. Just stick to them and then you will earn your daily walk outside with the others. But you need to be patient. It won't happen so quick."

He continued to eat, and Jack kept on watching him. "Any issues, let me know. I am here and will be checking up on you regularly as of evenings."

"Thank you, Jack, very kind of you."

Michael slowed down eating, as he did not want to finish so quickly. After all, he had nothing else to do. The fact that the guard kept watching him made him a bit nervous. He was not sure what it meant. It was difficult to just ignore him.

As Jack continued to keep his eyes transfixed on Michael, he went for another refill. Eventually he heard the sliding window being pushed across. The guard had left. He listened to the footsteps behind the door getting dimmer, until there was no further sound at all. There was nothing but silence, and total stillness reigned.

Michael looked again at the massive door and then peeked out of his window, while he finished his last bit of fruit. He chewed it slowly to let time pass. He had a lot of it now, he knew. He then placed everything very neatly on the tray, but kept the cup, and walked to the door. He carefully placed his tray in front of the hatch and turned towards his window again. He was not feeling tired even though he had not slept at all the last few days. Too much tension had been building up and it had not been released due to the unfavorable verdict.

He put a pillow under his head and rested, lying on his bed with his face towards the window. Looking out at the dark sky he wondered how his first night in prison would turn out. There were no noises, just an eerie quietness. He kept peering out at the black sky, occasionally drifting off and then coming back to his cell. Before Michael realized it, it was early morning and the sky lit up. He knew it would soon be breakfast time. He looked over his shoulder and saw that the tray had gone. He must have been asleep after all; he had not heard it being taken. Another day of loneliness, full of thoughts and worries needed to go by until evening. Then Jack would also reappear for his night shift at the window opening of his cell door, and they could converse again.

Many nights and weeks followed. Jack regularly appeared at the observation window engaging him for hours. He did not pose a lot of questions and let Michael do the talking. Whenever Michael asked about his personal life, the answers remained vague, and were twisted instead into more questions about his own past. Initially he had a lot of apprehension about speaking to Jack and wondered why he spent so much time at night chatting to him. With time though, Michael got used to it. He presumed that also other inmates received similar attention. It was important for him to be able to talk to someone other than himself. Loneliness and not knowing what to do and being on his own all day without any contact during his first weeks gave him more trouble than he had expected.

Even though he still had a certain uneasiness to open up to Jack and remained wary of his intentions, over the weeks that followed, he grew more comfortable with his presence. Michael tended to chat away, telling Jack about his life, when he was small and how he used to go scouting. He even became a leader and was named Skipper. He told stories about his interests as he grew up and as he became older, how he longed for other pleasures and started the triathlon. He also wanted to do Ironman one day, which consisted of 3.8 km swimming, 180 km biking and then a marathon. Finding time was the issue. You needed a lot of it for training, which he did not have when he went to university. But he continued still the three sporting exercises on a smaller scale and entered a half triathlon one day. It was only 1.9 km swimming, during which he struggled a bit. Swimming was not his strong point, but he still managed to pull through. Then it was 90 km on the bike, on an unfortunate day in the pouring and freezing rain. Finally, then a half-marathon, 21 km, which he finished soaking wet and shivering. He had been simply glad to complete the race and swore never to take part again. He continued running though. Now and then he also joined friends in the gym to pump some iron; Michael was in particularly good physical shape.

"So, you became a runner then and kept fit, that is good." Jack was all interested in keeping the conversation running.

"It was a good balance to my studies at university. When you are ploughing over your books all day, you need to let out some energy, so I went often for a long run in the evenings to clear my head." A moment of silence passed, as Michael thought about how to keep the discussion going. "Do you do any sports, Jack?"

"Not really. I am more of a walker. I spend my nights here, sleep till one in the afternoon, sometimes two, and spend most of the day strolling around town till it becomes late. It is my way to get my share of exercise, and I prefer it this way."

Michael nodded as he sat with his back against the wall. After a while of stillness, he remembered how long he had now been incarcerated. "Tomorrow it is three months I am here, Jack, so I suppose I am allowed to go outside?"

"That's right. I was going to tell you; I saw it in the warden's book. Tomorrow morning after breakfast you will be called. Stay calm and relaxed, it will be fine. There is nothing to worry about."

"Great, I am looking forward to it. I am longing to get out of here to catch some fresh air, finally."

"Well, you deserve it, Michael, you certainly do. Have fun. See you tomorrow and tell me all about it."

"Good night, Jack. Thanks again for dropping by."

The window shut and Michael was again on his own but feeling quite jolly. How much a person could become happy with so little, he only realized now. This little joy of being able to leave his cell and go outside meant a lot to him. He lay down and watched the sky again from his bed and soon fell asleep, dreaming of past times, scouting with his friends, marching the forests and being free, free to roam and do what he wanted.

CHAPTER 3

A Game of Chess

Michael had already spent three months as a prisoner getting used to his limited routine of life behind bars. Three times a day the hatch opened, and a tray was pushed through the bottom. Three to four times a week he was allowed to shower. He was given a bar of soap and a towel, which he was allowed to keep to take back to his cell, together with a fresh jumpsuit and dark socks. Otherwise, he spent most of his time sleeping to make time pass away. There were days he slept up to 15 hours, waking up and closing his eyes again, just to shut out his situation of total desperation. It was the only thing to do that would unburden him from his thoughts and anguish, as during waking hours his mind found little stillness, occupied with the new situation he had to face in life. Michael was depressed; he was not able to accept his situation, that he was sentenced for a crime he had not committed. Some nights he lay awake, trying to recollect the memories of that fatal encounter with Flynn Meier; but the harder he tried the more he got confused, as he was not able to add any further information to the pattern of events. Other nights he slept agitated, his mind racing during his sleep, constantly in pursuit of the unattainable truth of what could have happened, prior to his discovery of the body. Then he woke up, drenched in sweat, his heart pumping fast.

This morning he would be allowed to leave his cell. It was after breakfast, so Michael sat there impatiently and waited for the door to open. Finally, he would be given the opportunity to leave the room to get some fresh air and to hopefully meet other inmates.

As he sat there waiting, his mind drifted away to his parents. He was an only child, and they spent a lot of time together outside, often going for long hikes over the weekends. The news of his arrest had to be disclosed to them and they attended the last two days of the trial and, of course, the verdict. They did not take it well and the day he was sentenced, it was a harsh parting. The almost perfunctory wave of goodbye by his mother, while his father tried to leave the courtroom hurriedly, pulling her hand. He wanted to ensure they made it out of court before anybody could confront them. They had abandoned him out of shame for the sin he had committed. It was the last time he had seen them. Any scratch at his cell door jolted him up, in the hope of a visit. But up to today there had not even been a letter nor any further communication. Many days and nights he wondered why his parents had left him all on his own to suffer. He was devastated and in the dark hours he lay awake as tears covered his face. He had not expected this, especially not from his beloved mother.

As Michael thought about her, the image of Eileen popped up in his mind. Eileen Parker was her full name. She was probably a bit younger than his mother, and she reminded him very much of her, due to the remarkably similar facial traits; the upturned nose, and the shiny dark eyes. She also had long brown, straight hair and the same calm, melodic and attractive voice. She wore tight jeans and a cream sweater, dressed just the way his mother did, when he saw her at the trial. Eileen was the only witness called by the defense. She was beautiful, and she had class. She explained that she worked nights at a bar nearby and was walking back home after work. She saw somebody passing by, running and panting, from the direction of the scene.

Michael initially felt relieved listening to Eileen's statement, as her positive appearance had the potential to impress both the jury and judge and make her testimony credible. However, his relief was short-lived.

The prosecution was led by Frank Wells. He was detailed, fierce, had an excellent memory and was extremely convincing. His preparation for trials was always meticulous and hence he seldom lost a verdict. Michael often wondered if Vincent was a worthy opponent; it was like a rookie battling against the veteran. Frank Wells fired his questions at Eileen so quickly that at times she seemed lost, not able to respond, too overwhelmed by the situation. He knew how to play his cards and used his terrain well after many years of experience questioning people. Court cases were battles, and the more convincing party often won.

Eileen's positive appearance was quickly outweighed as she appeared very insecure up against the presence of an intimidating prosecutor and a stern looking and towering Judge Carter. She was treated very harshly and came across as an unreliable witness. She tried to give a description of the person she saw, but she remained quite vague. The prosecution tried to discredit her, questioning her ability to remember what she had really seen. It was a one-sided questioning, with a fatal ending. When asked if she had something to drink during the evening, she admitted to having been offered a glass of champagne by a customer before going home. The prosecutor did not even question her state of sobriety, but simply concluded that she was drunk, as she had likely more than one drink during her working hours. Frank Wells kept repeating that she was not in any reasonable state to remember anybody. The judge never intervened, and Vincent never objected. Vincent did little to preserve any credibility of the witness and did not want to upset an already angry judge by objecting to the assumption of Wells. He knew Judge Carter would never sustain this. Michael felt completely let down.

Before Eileen was dismissed, the prosecutor provided his highlight of the interrogation by confidently approaching the jury. They watched attentively as Frank Wells stood tall, with a convincing smile, and hung onto every word he articulated in a clear manner. He took off his glasses, holding them in one hand and his script in his other.

"It is not unusual that people go out running at night. After all, the quality of the air during these hours is significantly superior to daytime. So perhaps Ms. Parker saw someone going for a jog?" He managed to extract a few laughs among the jury members.

The conclusion of the inquest was that the apparent jogger was never identified, and it was even questioned whether he existed. Judge Carter showed no sympathy. The case was quickly concluded. Michael was the only person at the scene, his prints matched, so he must have stabbed the victim. The jury unanimously voted for the maximum prison sentence proposed by Judge Carter, for assault and killing. When the court adjourned, Michael was taken straight away by two big police officers, escorted in handcuffs, out of the back of the room. They descended down to the basement, where he had to exit the building at the rear. Outside in a courtyard was a minibus with caged windows waiting, which took him right to this place.

Michael was jolted back to his present reality when he heard the lock activate a few times. The door suddenly opened. Finally, he was able to leave his cell. Followed by a friendly-looking guard, he was ordered to pass through different corridors and heavy doors, and then found himself at last in the open air in a huge courtyard, surrounded by high prison walls.

"Today is your first day out, so time will be a bit shorter. As of tomorrow, you will be a regular with the other inmates."

Michael did not care. He was simply relieved to be out. "Thank you, sir."

He ran his hand through his newly grown brown hair as he furtively looked around at his new surroundings. The first day he had entered, his head had been completely shaven. They explained that it was a precautionary measure against head lice.

Just a few guards stood benignly high above in a glass-enclosed guard room on one corner tower of the prison yard. They were relaxed and chatting away, as they knew that there was no chance of escape. The prison was recently built, with tall walls and movement sensors, so there was no possibility of any tunnel system, as the erection of the whole establishment was made on hard bedrock. All walls were constructed with steel fiber-reinforced concrete, these were fiber inclusions of steel, added to the matrix of concrete after mixing. Any scraping with primitive tools, to make a hole or a possible escape shaft, would be futile.

Michael, as in other new situations, was not quite sure how to behave, as he was still learning and adapting to life in a new world. It was like the first morning for a child coming to a new school in another city. Countless books he had read and films he had seen in his youth. Alcatraz was the most notable one that came to his mind at that moment. Gangs, territories. *Just stay out of trouble*, he thought to himself. And he was determined to do so. He wanted to mind his own business and not to invade anybody's domain. He strode carefully within the courtyard and wanted to simply enjoy the freshness of the air, something he missed dearly. He relished the moment and realized that the simplest and mundane gift of life can be appreciated. After three months being locked away, it was a great relief for him to walk in the open.

Michael took a deep breath and looked around. A cool breeze stung his face—he was not used to being outside anymore. It was a chilly morning for this time of the year, and he blew fake smoke clouds into the air, his warm breath condensing into many tiny droplets of liquid water, but then vanishing again, the same way as his hope for freedom vanished, the same way all support from friends or relatives had disappeared. He had not received a single visit since his stay.

The ground was evenly cemented with several benches scattered around the court, occupied by other prisoners. While he kept on taking deep profound breaths and exhaling slowly, he noticed that he was eyed upon by one inmate sitting on one of the benches. By his looks, Michael presumed of Latino origin. He was toying with a cigarette in his right hand and then held it up high, pointing to Michael. He had never smoked and had no desire to start here. He politely declined by holding up his hands and mouthing the words, "Thank you." Michael hoped that this would not be taken impolitely, nor did he want to come across as pusillanimous, cowardly, or showing any sign of weakness. So, Michael smiled confidently and nodded his head in appreciation, but moved on, not accepting the invitation.

Diverse groups of prisoners were scattered around. Some played ball, some walked around in small groups, others just sat there. In the far corner was a weathered wooden table with two chairs. One chair was vacant and on the opposite side someone was seated. He was looking down, his right elbow on the table, fingers supporting his forehead. It was the typical pensive mode of a person concentrating on a game. Michael continued to walk towards him, and his assumption proved him right. He was playing a game of chess against an imaginary opponent. He had the black pieces and the white ones on the other side.

When Michael stood next to him, he hesitantly said, "May I be White?"

The man did not move, nor did he look up. "Have a seat and make yourself comfortable. It's your turn. Queen F6 to C3 was my last move."

Michael took his place and quickly analyzed the positions of his white pieces. The black Queen was attacking him, and he had to watch out as the next move by Black would probably be Check. Michael had two possibilities, either to bring back his Knight F3 to E1 to avoid the Check, or to go for a counterattack with his Bishop. The next move by Black, allowing the black Queen to Check him would then simply be resolved by moving his white Rook back to D1, attacking the black Queen. His Rook would be protected by his second, adjacent Knight on E3. Michael was always audacious as a student, he liked to take chances, calculated chances, hence his interest also for blackjack. Chess was no different for him. Calculate your moves ahead, imagining what your opponent would do next. So, Michael took his Bishop, H3 to F5.

His opponent lifted his head, raised his eyebrows, and crossed his arms, placing them on the table in front of him. He leaned forward, still without looking up, and took a deep breath. "Nice move. Played a lot?"

"As a student in a chess club, when I had time."

The chess player finally lifted his eyes up and studied Michael. "You look pretty young. I haven't seen you around yet, you must have arrived not so long ago."

Michael sat back, placed his hands in his lap and looked at the man in front of him. He was likely somewhere in his thirties, he guessed. He was clean shaven, had bright blond hair and a friendly expression. Michael nodded and thought about what he was going to say. "Yeah, just got here, three months ago."

"So, your first time out then, must have behaved well."

"I guess."

"How much time?"

Michael looked down and reflected. He was initially hesitant to really say it aloud, as he had never mentioned the length of his stay to anybody. "*Twenty-six years,*" he responded almost inaudibly, looking back up, trying to catch the eyes of his chess companion. Twenty-six years? *Could that really be?* he thought.

The blond man jerked his head back, stunned. "Oh boy, you must have upset someone, badly! Nobody round here gets more than fifteen. Most of them get out after ten, on parole, if they behave."

Only ten years, Michael thought to himself.

"You cannot be a first or second-degree offender—there aren't any here in this place. At most, someone here killed somebody accidentally. It was not planned and there had been no intent, you understand?"

"How do you know so much about this?"

"I am a lawyer and I have my sources."

"A lawyer?"

"Yes, nothing unusual. And you?"

"I studied economics and started work as an accountant for the local tax office."

Tom looked back down while listening and executed his next move, taking his Queen back from C3 to C6, attacking Michael's white Rook. "What's your name?" Tom continued to study the pieces, awaiting his opponent's move.

"Michael, Michael Fletcher."

"I am Tom, Tom Bane."

"Pleasure to meet you." Michael lifted his hand and wanted to shake Tom's.

Tom looked up and shook his head. "Better not, not here. It may be seen as a deal or something similar. Better to keep your head down, then you will be fine and make it through. The less physical contact, the better."

"Yes, Tom, thanks for the advice."

"You will learn, don't worry. It is not that bad here. Most of us just want to get out again. We did something stupid, and we are just sitting time, nothing else. Just remember, going down is easy, but getting up is hard. Hang in there and don't get caught in anything. Stick to the rules, do not upset anybody, and make sure to mind your own business."

Michael listened to the fatherly advice he seemed to get and contemplated his next chess move. Tom's words came back to him repeatedly. *Must have upset someone, badly.* He was not sure how to digest the comment of Tom and tried to refocus on the game, while his mind kept swirling with the remark he had received. *What did Tom mean by this? Did I get more years than anyone else who came here? Why was that?* Michael continued playing the game but lost his concentration. His brain was just somewhere else, trying to understand the significance of Tom's words.

"Checkmate."

Michael nodded. "Well done, Tom, you made the better moves, looks like we need to do a rematch tomorrow. Okay for you?"

"Sure. I am taking the board with me and will be here again tomorrow, for the next twelve, or if I am lucky, only ten years."

"Thank you, Tom, I appreciate it." He wondered how a lawyer ended up in prison. Tom hadn't asked him either what he had done. Maybe another day the conversation would come up. It was only the first time they had met, and he was also unsure whether committed crimes were really discussed.

Tom frowned and observed his new acquaintance sadly, leaning back. He ran his right hand heavily across his chin, as if trying to feel his stubble, while regarding him intensely, squinting his eyes slightly. "I really wonder who you pissed off. Must have been someone important. Never tried to find out?"

Surely, he had asked himself why the punishment was so severe, and he also wanted to understand it from his attorney, Vincent Graham. The explanation remained vague and no time at all was spent after the trial on any analysis. As quickly as Vincent appeared the first day, he was also gone just as quickly. Everything went so fast, with little counsel and help. There had been nobody else for his support. The moment he was arrested it was a situation of disbelief for him. He was not really himself. Beaten morally and accused of crime, from the first hearing to the moment he found himself on the bus to prison. It was as if living in a trance. Michael was about to respond as a whistle blew.

"Good to meet you Michael, better go immediately, otherwise there is trouble. Keep your head up and don't do anything stupid. Not here, you will regret it."

Thanks for the advice, Michael nodded over his shoulder as he headed swiftly for the entrance gate, back into the building.

"See you tomorrow," Tom called after him, putting the last pawn into a black cotton bag.

CHAPTER 4

The Meaning of Life

Everyone was escorted away to their cages in groups. Michael walked ahead and stopped at sliding doors, which opened and then closed, after the guards had passed them. He turned corners and stopped obediently when told to do so. After a few minutes he found himself again in front of his cell door, which he realized had Roman symbols stamped on the very top in thick black letters. XLIX, number 49. He knew the Roman letters, and the L stood for 50, the X for 10 and the I for one. The X before the 50 meant that it was 50 minus 10, so 40. Romans did not put four characters of the same symbol together. He always wondered why they did not just write VIIII to say nine. His teacher told him once that they call it subtractive numerals, making it simply less letters by writing IX.

Michael was back inside. He had a lot to think about and he had plenty of time. He rested on his bed and thought about his first breath of air for three months, the Latino offering him a cigarette, the game of chess, every moment of the time he passed outside, the way back to his cell door, up until the moment he saw the Roman letters. The words of Tom kept ringing in his ears. *Must have upset someone badly. Nobody 'round here gets more than fifteen.* Why him then, why did he get more than the others?

Was it the judge he had upset and was this the reason he had shown so little sympathy during the trial?

His mind was still occupied with the unidentified person who Eileen had seen running. Who was he, and why hadn't anybody tried to identify this mysterious person any further? Every day he prayed that another witness came forward to reopen his case. If that person were really doing any nighttime exercise, he may have also seen something significant, something that could have exonerated Michael. He pondered on what Eileen had said, more than once, but his mind kept running in circles. The judge stated that the evidence was not strong enough and he would have to dismiss her. Her account was too weak; it lacked description.

So many questions popped up and Michael could not find a way to put them into a pattern to make some sense out of it. He couldn't shake the feeling that there was more than just a standard trial that decided his fate. While he sat on his bed looking at his toilet, sink, white walls, and the shelf that was now filled with a few personal items, he felt the same knot again in his stomach. It was the very same pain he'd had just three months ago, when he first entered his cell. He shook his head and realized he would never accept what had happened to him. Why should he? He had not done injustice, not to his best collection. He was stuffed away into this small room, bereft of any pleasure of normal life, despite supplicating to Vincent, the judge, and the jury that they believe in his innocence.

Michael passed much of his days in solitude and suffering. The only thing that gave him some peace of mind were his three hours outside, spending time walking around or playing the occasional game with Tom. Being able to work also in the library, the laundry or even in the kitchen was a welcome way to make the hours tick away. Anything really to make the days seemingly shorter helped him to survive his stay. Nights were peaceful and the routine visits of Jack became a habit that Michael appreciated highly. Discussions were deep and he was able to get things off his chest that bothered and worried him.

Michael continued to tell stories about his life, sometimes for hours in the dark of the night. Jack, who let out one night that his surname was Feller, always peered through the observation window, which slid across the upper part of the door. Michael started from his childhood, what he did, when he went to university and then how he ended up in town, starting his first job. Michael's confidence grew and he confided more in Jack by the day. He tried to prompt him often with questions, however, Jack continued to avoid any details about his family life. He wondered why and was still curious as to why Jack spent so much time in the middle of the nights speaking to him, always through that little opening. He found his resemblance hard to imagine. All he saw were these bright blue eyes, sparkling through that square hole and a very appealing deep voice accompanying them. It was Michael doing most of the talking. Jack remained furtive about his past, but as the years ticked by and their conversation got more intimate, he one day had the courage to ask Jack more directly.

"Please, tell me, Jack. Why did you become a guard? Was being a police officer not so good?"

There was a long wait. He cranked his head and saw the blinking blue eyes, then listened, waiting for a response. It occurred often that they did not converse. At times minutes passed, as Jack just stood there not uttering a single word, while he lay there on his back, watching the ceiling, also contemplating what to say next. This night as well, a long quietude grew and filled the air. Once again, he looked up to check if Jack Feller was still there, when finally, the silence was broken.

"You see, Michael, I wanted to quit my job, to do something else. I was not comfortable anymore with crime scenes. I could have gone to parking enforcement or traffic and so on, but then there was a position here, working nights. Good pay actually, due to the nighttime shift. Although the hours for this job may not be preferred by many, I actually enjoy it. One of the benefits is that while others are working during the day, I am free. At night I do my inspection rounds and read my books. This prison is so secure with all these technologies, anything wrong and the alarms go off automatically. You could basically run it without personnel at these hours," he said very quietly. "Yeah, saw the opening, applied and got the job straight away."

"Well, I am glad you are here. You are giving me company. I wonder what you look like. I just see your eyes."

Another silence passed when Jack whispered, "I am on my own here at nights. You need to wait a few more years. Can't really let you out, you know, internal rules. Imagine if something happened when somebody was allowed out of his cell at night. That really makes this place so different to all other prisons. It is not possible to pass the doors; everybody is securely locked away." A few more minutes passed, and Michael peered across again to see if Jack was still there. "I do not do day-duty. So, you will know, one day, what I look like."

"One day, Jack, yes, one day, time must pass. You cannot imagine how hard it is for me. I already told you my story, and you believe me, you said so. So, you must understand what it is like for me, and what I am going through day by day."

"I do, Michael. Believe me, I do."

Michael adjusted relatively well to prison life as he got used to all the routines. He met new inmates, but a lot of his days were spent on his own, often glaring out of the window. The question he posed himself was: *What is the point of life?*

Possibly (1) to be born and to explore one's passions and interests, to make the most of the time we have on this planet, and (2) to overcome challenges and obstacles in life to simply survive, and (3) to leave a lasting legacy, to do something that people will remember you for after you have died.

"Well, I guess the latter two I have already achieved," he said to himself mockingly but sadly. He spoke often to himself, loudly. It was important for him to simply talk. "I just need to find a passion and to do something interesting." He still had a lot of time left to spend in jail. He therefore needed to pass the next years with a sense of purpose. He had no other option than to look positively ahead. If he crumbled now, he knew he would not make it through. He needed to remain strong.

Days, months and finally years continued to pass in prison. As hard as it was, Michael tried to maintain a positive mindset. He set up his daily routines and engaged in regular physical workouts, reducing stress and anxiety, which also improved his mood. He kept respectful relationships with other inmates by simply staying polite, but always with a hint of skepticism and keeping a certain distance. Michael was intelligent; he knew what to say and which controversial conversations to avoid. Any discussions on politics or religion he ignored, as he knew these were topics that could lead to heated arguments. If they came up, he remained smart by just showing interest in other opinions, without expressing his.

Michael tried to spend as much time as he could working in the library. He sorted, read many of the books and knew what categories they all belonged to. He found great joy in also advising other inmates on a good read, and soon received the nickname "professor." He always smiled and took it as a compliment. Books intrigued him and he was always proud when others thanked him for his advice. Michael understood that apart from enhancing knowledge and preparing you for a better life with more opportunities, reading had another significant importance, especially in prison; it stimulated his brain to prevent any mental decline.

One day when collecting a book, Michael was greatly impressed as an inmate asked him to sit down for a moment to talk about the meaning of the novel. The professor listened and was able to exchange a few words discussing what they had just read. These more profound exchanges, Michael realized, improved empathy greatly. Apart from the usual frivolous conversations, more meaningful discussions were held. He had a sensation that stress levels were greatly reduced. Frustration was a big issue among prisoners, as being locked away with little hope was a constant trigger for outbursts of aggression.

Alcohol was not allowed and there was truly little possibility to gain access. The only way to get something from the outside was through visitors. Any relatives were searched and scanned, so it was quite impossible for any liquid to enter. Michael did not mind; after his fateful episode on a drunken night which brought him here, he had no desire for anything but water. Some of the inmates were led astray by smaller drug problems. These were smuggled in smaller doses through random gifts, but the quantity remained negligible.

Everyone could regularly visit the barber shop for shaving and haircuts. The rule was that you needed to keep yourself clean and properly groomed. Michael did not want to violate this and neither wanted to face the wrath of his fellow prisoners. No rules were made about hair length, as long it was neat, so he decided also to adopt the approach of not too short and not too long. He wanted to simply not be noticed. All inventory was always carefully eyed upon by an officer; he kept a constant watch over every activity. At the end of the day, all tools were counted and locked away.

Michael continued to reevaluate his life over the years. He read books about psychology that kept repeating that it was important in life to embrace your problems rather than run away from them. As difficult as it was it helped him. He accepted his incarceration and was also soon to find a new important purpose.

CHAPTER 5

The Years Pass By

After fifteen years of life behind bars, Michael had the desire to return to a regular life, so he decided to put in his first request for an early release. The hope of contesting his sentence had long gone. He was trialed and incarcerated, and this was the bitter fact he had accepted. His only hope that remained was to try to shorten his suffering as much as possible.

He borrowed as many law books from the library as he could find and spent hours in his cage reading them. He wanted to better understand what he could do to achieve an early release. Years back, he also relied on Tom Bane, his chess partner, hoping to receive some legal advice. Certain consultation was offered, but Michael could not explain it exactly . . . he felt a certain reticence on behalf of Tom. Tom had been set free five years ago and had wished Michael all the best. Before Tom left though, they met one last time at the same table, with the same chess board. It was one of the most memorable conversations he'd had in years. Tom had explained that he was terribly sorry for Michael's situation and confessed that he did not really try his best to help him. Michael recalled well the exchange he had. He recalled it as if it had happened this morning, so significant it was, and would turn out to be for him one day.

As they sat for the last time together outside, Tom rubbed his face, peeked right and left, and started his discourse. "Michael, do you have any idea what the cost of an average prisoner is per year?"

"I have no idea; depends on the prison I guess."

"Absolutely right. Can be anywhere between fifty thousand to a hundred thousand or even more per prisoner per year. High security, low security, you name it. The budget for this one was officially on the much lower side, plus the cost of building it, of course. Now guess how much the mayor promised it would cost?"

"Why are you telling me this?"

"You better listen carefully now, to what I am trying to convey. This prison was almost self-funded. Paid for by taxes, by all the companies constructing this. You are an economist; you can do the math. Almost zero interest for funding this place is paid back over the years through taxes by the companies who built this thing and those who maintain it. Jobs are created and everyone is happy. It is an extremely clever model."

"So?"

"Apart from almost self-funding the building, running this prison costs less than half of the initial budget per year. You know why? Security and health care account for by far the biggest cost of managing prisons, security being the largest share of these two. These costs were more than halved. You know how? Almost no security. Ever wondered why only Jack Feller is roaming around at night, all on his own?"

Michael shook his head. "Never thought about it."

"Listen, this is not a standard prison. Okay, you have convicts like you and me, who made a mistake. We did something unlawful, made a bad choice. But we are not considered as felons that will remain criminals for life. It is expected, when someone from this place gets out, they will live a normal life again. They want to make it possible for everyone here to reenter into society, referred to also as *full reintegration*. Look at me: I have a wife and a girl; she is cute and everything. Tomorrow, when I am out, it will be still in time for her to call me 'daddy.' I am guaranteed a job and reinstatement as a normal citizen. Do you know what the word *expunge* means?"

"Yeah, I do. It's to erase something completely."

"Exactly! My criminal record will even be expunged. That means my conviction is destroyed or sealed from the federal records. This whole institution is a pilot project."

Michael nodded and Tom continued, looking around for any eavesdroppers. "As you can see, the prison is new, and the security is low. There was this big incentive by the mayor, I can't remember his name. Anyway, the incentive was to reduce public spending, so it is he who put this initiative in place a long time ago, right at the beginning of his career. He even overlooked the construction of this damn place. He had won the election by a landslide. He promised to put more money into public spending for schools, education, recreational facilities, and parks, by reducing the expenses for this prison."

"Okay, so where are you heading in this discussion?"

"Michael, I was transferred here from another place, like almost all of us. We arrived together a couple of months before you came. This place was brand new when we entered. As I just said, Michael, this is a pilot project, a low security place; they are educating us to be good and are only putting criminals here that have a lesser tendency for violence. They feed us well, it is clean, and we all stay healthy, so there is also an exceptionally low cost of healthcare here. Anybody causing trouble though is gone, the very first day, no questions asked, and he is sent to a high security prison somewhere else. Nobody who comes here wants to risk this. This is a nice place to be and the prospects when getting out are more than good. We are basically prepared when we get outside. You know what a rabbit is?"

"I assume you don't mean the animal with two long ears?"

Tom smiled. "Yes, not them. It is basically someone who has tried to escape. You won't find either of these here. That is why there aren't any rabbits. If anyone tries, they are gone as well. This is supposed to be the model prison of the entire country. You cannot imagine how the mayor boasts in town about how nicely this place is being run, with extremely low costs. He has so little expenses, that he is now able to fulfill his promise made for public spending on all other things."

Michael scratched his head and repeated his question. "Tom, what are you trying to tell me here, on your last day?"

"What I am saying is that this prison and the whole justice system is in the hands of someone really powerful." Tom breathed in again, nervously looking around. "I told you that there is something about your case that seems amiss. Why should you get fifteen or sixteen years more than anybody else here and be thrown into a place like this with us? Ever thought about it? Nobody here gets more than ten years to fulfill the model prisoner life. But you? Why are you here? All I am telling you is that there is someone with a lot of influence out there that gave you your sentence and threw you in here, to also keep an eye on you. It is also clear that the second-degree murder charge was never justified. Your whole trial was a farce. I am sorry I am telling you this only now. The point I am getting at is that I did not do everything I could during my stay to help you, as I would have been otherwise playing with fire. I did not want to get dragged into this and cause any trouble. I wanted to simply get out. I was afraid my sentence may not be reduced. But once I am out though, I promise to do some digging."

It was shocking to hear this from the mouth of someone he considered a friend and trusted fully up to that point. Tom had hidden something important all these years and could have likely helped him. Michael replayed the conversation he'd had with Tom many times and pondered upon the meaning of the word friendship. He had seen a few movies about life in prison and what came to his mind most notably was *The Shawshank Redemption*. The important meaning of the movie, at least for Michael, was that it was possible for a real friendship to evolve; one that lasted up to the grand ending when they met up again at the beach. Michael had seen it for the first and only time just months before his arrest. It was the most notable film that remained in his memories. He decided to tread carefully from now on. The significance of playing chess with Tom he only understood now.

It was also just a few days after Tom was released that one morning when Michael woke up, he found a brand-new chess board lying next to the hatch with a small note on top of it. *Now that Tom is out, I hope you continue playing. Now you have your own board.* There was no name, but it could have only been from Jack. He was grateful for this gift. He took it outside on many occasions and sat at the same table he used to sit with Tom for years, playing along against different opponents. Tom had sat a full ten years out of twelve; two years were dismissed for good behavior.

Michael pondered again on the term friendship and its profound meaning as he sat in his cell, taking the bishop in his hand and studying it. This bishop had been loyal and protected its queen and king now for five years. He had developed a friendship with Jack. As important it was for him, he was uncertain if he could really consider Jack a friend, even though he was the only person with whom he could share his worries and feelings—the only person he really trusted. To which extent he was not sure; he was, after all, a guard. Michael therefore decided not to touch upon the topic of parole and his studies of the law books.

Michael read and reread all the possible books he had. One of the books confirmed what Tom had said. Before a "petition could be filed, a minimum period of the sentence had to be served." Tom had advised him against trying to ask for an early release too soon, as it was simply premature to do so. He therefore waited patiently and continued to study his possibilities long after Tom had left.

By filing a motion for early parole, Michael read, a skilled attorney was needed. Vincent was his only hope. But he had not heard from him for years. So, he went about filing his own petition for early parole eventually. He had served many years already, and the time to file a motion had come. In books, he read that a parole is granted whenever a board finds that there is a reasonable probability that if released, the convicted person will become a law-abiding citizen. Michael had no intention of doing otherwise. Furthermore, a good conduct time also gave the possibility of reducing the sentence. Michael had the view that he had earned this further allowance, as he had never caused any trouble during his stay.

According to the books, the decision would be taken out of the hands of the prison officials and placed before a judge. However, which judge, he did not know. If presented again to Judge Carter, the person who so despised him during trial, would he really grant him parole?

Michael tried many successive years. The request was never granted during his entire stay. The fact that the demand was simply rejected in writing was what struck him most. Michael read about the possibility of at least getting a chance to present himself to a parole board. However, it never went that far. As he unfolded the A4 paper, all he saw were three lines rejecting his petition. It was all he got; no further reasons were provided. Michael turned over the page several times, hoping to find something on the other side. But no matter how often he turned the page, it was always the same three lines. He had kept his last two letters under his mattress. They were identical; just the date had changed, as if they had all been written by the same person. Michael recalled when applying after university for jobs frequently using the same format on his personal computer, for the same type of letter. All he did was change the date and the addressee. It seemed to him that here the same person opened the same file and printed it on the same printer with identical paper.

Michael was one of the few, if not the only, graduate in prison that remained after Tom had left. His chess partners changed often, as most of them only wanted to play because they were curious. Nobody had a real passion for the game. It was a thinking sport and needed a great deal of concentration. He had been playing now for over fifteen years constantly, every day, and he became exceptionally good at it. Even on nights when the moonlight shone through the window, he got up and played against an imaginary opponent, the same way Tom Bane had done, when he saw him first. None of the inmates had studied; many had not even completed school. Most of them complained that the mathematics was too difficult, a comment at which Michael smirked. He was an excellent mathematician. Of course, statistics, as an economist, was more his strength than anything else, but he understood it all pretty well. Fernando had asked once if Michael could help him, and he had accepted at once.

Fernando was of Spanish origin and a school dropout. He came from a wealthy family which did not have the time really to look after him. His parents were successful businesspeople, roaming the world, selling luxury yachts. Fernando did not receive the right support at home and decided to go abroad to try his luck. A big sum of money was given to him by his busy father as a present. Fernando was just eighteen years old when he left and soon spent everything he had. His lack of education showed its signs; he did not know how to look after his financials. He was still in his teens when he stupidly got involved in a bank robbery. He was convinced by the town gang to come along. He had no job and was short of cash. A nice slice of the cake was promised. It all went (of course) not as expected. Fernando did not even know how to handle a gun properly and accidentally shot a customer who panicked. The woman stayed in intensive care for four days, when finally, the doctors could not save her anymore. Fernando was charged with murder. His father was a devoted Catholic and prayed for his son every day. He was so devoted that he absolved him from his sins and promised, once exonerated, to welcome his prodigal son back home again when he got out. Fernando was so emotional that he cried in his parents' arms. Both mum and dad hugged him tightly before he was taken away. He was sorry for what he had done. He promised them that one day he would join his father's business. His parents returned home and awaited the day their son would return. They visited him often.

It was a sentimental story for Michael with mixed feelings. On the one hand, he had received all the support from his parents up to life after university, while Fernando had not. He understood that a stable and supportive family was the basis to stay out of trouble. On the other hand, now his parents had deserted him, while Fernando had been absolved by his family for his wrongdoings.

Michael felt pity and was allowed to spend time in the library teaching Fernando the basics of mathematics and other important subjects to prepare him to finish his school exams. It was a service that the prison provided, another initiative by the mayor in his campaign, to give the convicted the possibility to complete school or any other further education. The better their education would become, the easier the integration. Michael spent many months, which turned into years, not just teaching Fernando but also other detainees his skills. Exams could be sat during the year, and he turned out to become a quite proficient teacher. His name as a real professor made the rounds. All his students passed. Some did not achieve good grades, but all of the ones he taught made the exams. A strong handshake was the reward when they left prison, when their sentence had been completed, and personal satisfaction of the teacher. Michael watched them come and go. He had to serve the longest. On the day of Fernando's release, he went to see his teacher. He thanked Michael dearly and promised to get in contact one day. He was going to work immediately in export, travelling, in his father's business. He also intended to go to study one day. Thanks to Michael's devotion he completed school in prison with excellent results, mathematics even with distinction.

Michael discovered encouragement through helping others, resulting in a deep sense of personal fulfillment and accomplishment. He was intrigued by the situation of fellow prisoners and learned that much of their imprisonment was due to their lack of support in life; they were simply led astray. Michael studied as much as he could with other inmates; he understood that helping them with their education would be their only way into a better post-prison life. Michael had found a new purpose within his difficult existence.

Jack kept visiting regularly at night and Michael reported proudly how he had helped many of his fellow inmates to pass their exams. Jack encouraged him to continue, as it would make time pass faster in prison. However, in the final years of Michael's confinement, there were nights when Jack did not appear. For one period Michael didn't see him for weeks. He gave no explanation, but just turned up again and spoke as if he had been there yesterday. Although Michael was tempted to inquire about the reasons behind Jack's prolonged absences, he ultimately chose to accept them as a regular occurrence during his final years of incarceration. Only later, one day, would the real reason reveal itself.

The years went by, and Michael became older. He was twenty-five when he entered and would be fifty-one when the last day of his incarceration arrived. Michael was longing for an end to his time in prison, to get out and to start a completely new life. He had counted down the years and the end of his prison sentence had come. Time had ticked by. *Just a few more days*, he said to himself as he lay on his bed looking at the ceiling, imagining what he would do when released.

CHAPTER 6

Outside

Michael had finished his sentence and could soon leave as a free man. No early release and no parole had been granted over the years. He had always behaved impeccably and had longed for ease from detention. He would not have cared if it had even been under supervision. He had no interest in drugs or alcohol, he would have probably found himself a job; he had, after all, a university degree. He would have complied with the probation rules and seen the offender manager to receive counselling. He did everything possible to get out earlier, but it was to no avail.

His official release was just a week away, and there wasn't much for him to pack. Most things from his apartment were stored away somewhere in a warehouse. There was also that box he left, inside a bag with a few belongings and his clothes, when he entered this place many years back. What he intended to take with him was certainly the chess board that Jack had given to him sixteen years ago. Soon he would be out, and he expected that there was nobody beyond the prison gate to see him. Even his own family had disowned him twenty-six years ago; they distanced themselves from the very beginning. The day he had been condemned, an assertive newspaper reporter was present, taking notes meticulously in his booklet. When the sentence was announced by Judge Carter and Michael was taken away in his handcuffs, he quickly took a photo of Michael being escorted away. The picture made the front page of the town's gazette. Michael knew this and prayed that it remained a local news edition and would not spread across the country to parts where he was known, and his family lived. His father had always been strict and disciplined, working hard in life to become a successful district politician. His mother was more the soft and joyous part of the family, working as a schoolteacher and also as the principal of the school. His parents were hence immensely popular and well known, with a lot of important connections. What scandal and gossip would have arisen if a murder had been connected to their life. They decided to detach themselves from the day he was sentenced. He had hence never received a single visit from them. There was likely no family waiting for him outside.

This made it all the more surprising when Jack came one evening just one week before his official release.

"Michael, tonight is my last day of work. Tomorrow I will be retiring. You will be out next week."

"Yes, another seven days. I know. So, this is the last time we speak?"

"Well, not really. I wanted to ask if you'd like me to pick you up next week."

Michael needed a while to digest what had just been proposed and did not respond.

"As I said, I am retiring now, got not much to do, and perhaps we can continue talking when you are out. You can stay at my place for a while, no problem. I assume you have nowhere to go?"

Michael was baffled, trying to find the right words. The last thing he had expected was that Jack would propose something like this. He had been truly kind to him all these years and had become a precious person to be able to communicate with. However, he would have never imagined that Jack would have proposed something so considerate. Michael had wondered for many months during the final stages of his stay what he would do, and where he would go, when he got out. He considered visiting his parents, or simply disappearing abroad, searching for a new life, where nobody had ever heard the name of Michael Fletcher. He would get a job, maybe a girlfriend, start a new life. But this proposal stunned him.

"Well, I really do not know what to say—this is extremely generous and kind. Thank you, Jack. Very thoughtful of you, really, thank you so much."

"Good, so that is settled. I will see you then next week, on Monday, sometime after ten in the morning. You will exit through the main gate. I will be there waiting. I have a blue Prius."

"What is a Prius?"

Jack chuckled. "A Toyota. Don't worry, I will be standing next to a blue car." He realized that Michael probably would not even recognize the brand of the car. After twenty-six years, the world had changed. *This is going to be fun*, he thought to himself.

Michael lay awake most of the following nights. He was used to the sliding sound in the door behind his bed. A sound that had accompanied him for his entire stay. Without Jack, there was something missing, so used he had become to this custom. The days and nights seemed to pass slowly, so intense was his longing for his freedom now. He wondered often while watching the moon, his friend and companion over the years, whether Jack would really be there when he got out. The very last night, the night he had been waiting for so long, he doubted that Jack would keep his promise. *Well, at least you will be there every night for me again, won't you, my friend*, Michael whispered to the moon. He finally closed his eyes and fell asleep, still hearing the storm outside and the rain hitting his window.

The tempest that raged during the night had died down. It was a crisp Monday morning in early spring of 2022 as Michael stood on the doorway, peering out into a new world. He had aged little. His hair was still the same, no white streaks, and his skin as smooth as it had been the first day he came to this complex.

He inhaled and then stepped out of the same prison gate that he had entered a long time ago. He was dressed the same as twenty-six years ago, everything fitting perfectly. He had neither gained nor lost any weight. He was a bit more broad-shouldered from all the push-ups he had done over the years. The volume he gained in the shoulders, he lost in his torso. Lots of sit-ups had streamlined his belly. His face, though, was rather pale, almost white from a lack of direct sunlight. He let the breeze hit it while he closed his eyes and took a deep breath; his first real breath of freedom.

A gust of wind blew the remaining leaves of winter along the street as the sun peeked through the thin clouds. Michael did not have to look for long. He immediately saw somebody down the road waiving at him, standing next to a blue car. *Must be Jack Feller, who else would wave at me*. He had never seen Jack fully in person. All he knew were his eyes.

Jack stood there, smiling, as he approached him. He was also tall, maybe a bit smaller than Michael, in good condition. It was difficult to tell though due to a thick dark coat and a white scarf. His blue eyes shone at him the same way they had every night. It was the first time that Michael had really seen Jack standing in front of him fully, without that metal partition. He had thick black hair and looked healthy, with minor bags under his eyes and was grinning from ear to ear. His face was slightly tanned. He was exposed to daylight a lot, enjoying the sunshine. No surprise really for Michael. While others worked during the day, Jack probably was roaming around, enjoying himself.

Jack stuck out his hand and offered it. Michael took it hesitantly and shook it slowly. His hands were warm and soft. His smile was inviting and sincere.

"Welcome back to the outside world, Michael. I am happy you are out."

Michael did not quite know what to say or how to respond, so he just continued to shake his hand, looking at Jack and studying his complete face. He was overwhelmed and tried not to burst into tears. He was out, out at last. He took a deep breath, closed his eyes, and opened them again, just to make sure that he was really shaking the hand of Jack.

"Let me take this bag. I will just stick it in the trunk. Here, please get in," Jack laughed, letting go of Michael's hand with some difficulties, and then opening the door for him, "unless you want to drive? You got a license?"

"Yeah, I do, but I'll let you drive," Michael responded, as he watched Jack pushing a button on his key, the trunk opening alone without a human touch. His bag was stored away, and he got in on the passenger side and closed his door. The car smelled good, and the seat was extremely comfortable. There was a green felt pine tree hanging from the rearview mirror. *I smell good, but nature smells better*, was written in white letters on it.

Jack got in on the other side and looked at Michael. "Ready to go and start a new life?"

Michael looked from the tree to Jack and blew up his cheeks and breathed in heavily. Of course, he was. Where to, he was not sure, but he was certainly ready to be somewhere else.

"Yes, I suppose so," he exhaled finally.

"Well, better buckle up. We do not want to be stopped on our first day for any violation, do we?"

Jack looked at Michael and could not suppress a chuckle and a smile. He noticed that Michael took the humor well, even though the smile was not returned. He wondered when Michael had last experienced a moment of laughter. Was it something you could forget after living twenty-six years locked away?

Michael reached emotionlessly for the belt with his left hand, pulled it across his chest and pushed the latch into the buckle. As Jack started the car and pulled swiftly away, Michael looked furtively at him.

"I don't hear the engine."

"It is an electric car. Something new that came to the market a couple of years ago. They say it is better for the environment."

Michael looked across. "The environment?"

"Yeah, it is this new hype nowadays. You see, over the last few years more and more people are having this obsession about reducing emissions. They talk about global warming, how pollution is basically heating up the world."

"So, what's so bad about that?"

Jack scratched his chin with his left hand, while holding the steering wheel with his right.

"You see Michael, a lot has happened over the last twenty-six years. We've had more natural disasters than in the past. Many storms and floods but also the opposite like heat waves and droughts. There are lots of discussions. They argue about the melting of the polar caps, and even scientists quarrel about the subject and what the real causes are. One thing, however, that drives all this now, is our politicians. They of course jump on that train and do everything to impress the voters. If you ask me, it is only to get elected. Half of them do not even believe what they are saying. Some really do, I think, but often you see these politicians change their opinion, depending on what the majority of the people express. They swing one way or the other, because getting the votes matters. I certainly bought this car only because I got a good deal."

Michael cleared his throat and was about to say something, but then closed his mouth. He was too fascinated by his new surroundings. He gaped through the window like a little child merging into a new world—a world that had been hidden from him. The traffic was dense, almost bumper to bumper. He did not care. He was absorbed by the landscape, street signs, the shops and all the pedestrians scurrying along. For Michael it was as if he were on a sightseeing tour. All the changed scenery, and most notably the mass of people moving like ants in different directions. He simply admired all of it, something that had been denied to him for such a long time. A lot had changed and seemed so different than a quarter of a century ago.

In the city center Jack slowed down and eyed a gap between two cars. "Watch this. Look what happens when I push this parking assist button, here on the dashboard."

Michael focused as Jack pressed a panel button and all sorts of images started to appear on a screen that he initially interpreted as a small television. Jack let go of the steering wheel. Astonished, Michael stared as the wheel automatically turned one way and then the other, without Jack touching it, while the car moved slowly backwards, into the slot between the two cars.

"Fascinating, it's all automatic now? I had to learn to do this myself some time ago."

"You will be surprised how much more there is than last time you were outside. Technology has changed everything for the better, but, yeah, some of it I question myself, whether it is really necessary or good for us. You ever heard of the film *Terminator*?"

Michael thought for a moment. "Yeah, I recall the one with this Austrian actor. I watched the movie, actually I watched two. There was also a second one."

"Okay, there have been a few more since then. You know, all this control by artificial intelligence and machines taking over, you know them doing the thinking and all that, it has become increasingly realistic. Humanity has taken incredible steps over the recent years. I'll show you what I mean. I know this place where we can get something quick to eat. I guess you must be hungry."

They entered a quick-service restaurant and Jack went to a large screen where all types of burgers, fries and drinks popped up on the display when he touched it with his index finger.

"You see, here I can choose what I want, and also pay here with my credit card and sit down over there."

"Is this how you order today? Nobody to speak to?" Michael did not have to wait for long before a singing robot on two wheels ran along behind them, holding a tray with food. "Amazing! How does she know where to go, and what if someone is in her way?" Michael watched in fascination as the robot stopped at a nearby table and the customers took the tray. Then she spun around, came back, and disappeared behind a corner.

"In a lot of places there are still waiters. They exist still in most restaurants. I will take you to one tonight. This is simply faster; therefore, it is called a fast-food restaurant. Ha! Got the joke?" Jack nudged Michael with his right elbow and looked at him. Jack sensed that he managed to elicit a small smile across Michael's lips. He would need to try to work on that a bit more. He cared and wanted to make him feel better.

Michael continued glancing across the screen. "Sorry, I do not think my stomach will take this right now. After so much absence, can we have something lighter?"

Jack eyed him curiously. "You are right. I tell you what. Let us go easy on your tummy. How about I take you home and then I will cook something nice for you. You will definitely enjoy it. I am at the moment on this healthy diet trip and like to make fresh food. I guess you do not want to occupy the toilet for the rest of the day. You have been locked up long enough, eh? Sorry, bad joke." Jack grinned again, showing his teeth looking at Michael.

Michael did not respond. He knew Jack was simply trying to cheer him up. Eventually he would probably loosen up a bit, but it would take time.

As they left, Michael almost bumped into the high-pitched singing robot, which stopped instantly. He admired the sparkling eyes and how she held another tray full of food. He stepped aside and then the robot advanced to another table, where it stopped again. He continued to stare, like a little boy in a huge toy shop, all fascinated, marveling at all the gadgets. It was like arriving in a new world. "Welcome to the future," he said to himself.

Outside the restaurant, Michael stood still for a while before entering the car, observing everything around him. He had wondered for years how his new surroundings would have changed. Essentially, they were still the same, just more modern, cleaner, and certainly with many more flashing lights than he remembered.

CHAPTER 7

Home

They drove off again through the city and were very soon in the neighborhood, on a less busy road, approaching a bricked one-story bungalow with a double garage attached to the left. A patio and a small well-trimmed lawn decorated the front of the home. When Jack parked his car in his garage, which he opened and closed with the touch of a button, he got out and took a cable out of the boot. One end he fixed into the plug on the wall, and the other at the side to the car. Michael watched him curiously. He assumed that was the opening of the fuel cap, where you normally put in the petrol.

"One of these new things, Michael, we can also charge our cars at home, electric, you see!"

Michael was again impressed and wondered what more was to come.

"Come in, into my modest home unless you want to live in the garage?" Jack winked at him over his shoulder and entered through a wooden door that led into a short hallway. Here they hung up their coats, and from there moved directly into a large lounge.

"You can take my room here on the right. I can slumber on the couch. Most of the time I sleep there anyway. I watch TV and am too lazy to get up. Really no problem."

"Look, Jack, this is nice of you, but I'd be more comfortable taking the couch."

"Let us discuss it later. I will quickly pop into the kitchen and make something quick and healthy. If you want to shower, or use the bathroom, it is just here to the left."

Michael sat down on the cream leather couch and eyed the modishly furnished living room. It was essential, with a table, four matching chairs, the couch, and a huge TV one could watch while seated; he was taken aback by the size of it. There was a big wooden mahogany shelf in the corner with a large number of books, worn with use. Michael imagined Jack sitting in the guard room at night, feet up with a steaming coffee and reading them. He had probably read them over and over again. Michael seemed to recognize a few. He had read many from the prison library, but the occasional one was also pushed through the hatch by Jack. He had plenty of time to read and enjoyed it—it made time pass. After he had finished, he waited for the next night shift, thanked his lender, and pushed it back when the hatch opened. As Michael sat there in Jack's home and looked around, he realized the images of prison were still haunting him. He could not let go.

Michael looked out of the window, which had no curtains. Perhaps Jack would pull down some blinds in the evenings. He'd had none in his cell and had gotten used to the moonlight shining through the window at night. In prison, he turned around his cushion, so he was able to face the opening lying down. The moon kept him company. While watching the moon, time tended to pass faster, as the moon continued its trajectory in the sky. He estimated that it took about two hours for the moon to move from the left-hand part to the right-hand part of the window. It occupied him; two hours less in the long wait for freedom.

Once more his mind was playing tricks on him. He had to recollect himself; he was really here, in the home of Jack. To be able to fully realize, grasp and relish this moment of freedom would take time. He was finally out, but his conscience was not ready for it yet. He listened to the new sounds that had been hidden from him for such a long time. The occasional car passing outside, a clock ticking away on a table, and Jack chopping and sizzling away in the kitchen at the far end of the lounge. He heard a kettle roaring into life, a grinder rattle, and a humming noise of a kitchen fan. Michael sat there and simply admired his new stay. So friendly and welcoming, and much cozier than his previous one.

The room had a certain naked expression; it lacked a little warmth. He was wondering why it was different to the home he knew once upon a time when he was living with his parents, then he realized why. As he glanced around, he saw no plants, but what struck him most was that there were neither any pictures nor personal photos, just bare walls. Craning his head across, there weren't any on the shelf either.

"Got any family, Jack?" he shouted across the room. Jack had never talked about anything too personal and had never mentioned something about a family. In prison, he did not have the courage to pose the question directly in case he would have come across as impolite.

It was a moment before the answer came. "Yeah, I was married, got a small kid, a girl. However, I fell a bit apart with my wife's family, so one thing led to another. She left, even left me the house–nice of her–dad is a rich guy. Anyway, so now I live on my own. Luckily, I get to see my daughter every second weekend. I actually saw her yesterday. She's cute and she is the only real joy I have today. One day you will maybe meet her."

He continued to study the room while he heard his host clinking away in the kitchen. The lovely smell of fresh food being prepared made him hungry. He still expected, after so much time, that a hatch would open and that his food would be pushed through. But he was somehow taken back to reality when Jack came in with a big toothy grin. He held a huge tray with something to eat and a jar of water and placed it carefully on the table. He poured two glasses, dished out the plates and sat down. "Please come. Join me and let's eat."

Michael got up from the sofa and settled at the table, while Jack pushed a plate of toast with scrambled eggs, topped with spring onion and fresh seasonings, in front of him. Placed carefully around the border were freshly cut slices of avocado. Thin slices of lemon and sprinkled pepper gave the finishing touch. He admired his plate and picked up a set of cutleries while thanking Jack, before digging in. It looked delicious, smelled good and he had an appetite. He could not remember the last time he ate avocado. He could not even recall the last time he sat at a table and ate a meal with somebody.

Jack looked at him expectantly, grinning. "Enjoy, and do not rush. We have all the time now, to eat and chat away."

Michael took his first bite and then the next, slowly. He closed his eyes and relished the savor. "Thank you, Jack, this is wonderful."

Jack beamed and chewed away, then looked up. "So, Michael, what's on your mind, what are your plans, anything I can do for you?" Jack asked while munching.

He pondered for a moment while chewing and said, "Honestly, I don't really know. I mean, I must find a new purpose now. Do something interesting, maybe get a job, find a hobby, and get to know people. I thought about this hard the last few years, as I counted down my time. What shall I do when I am out? There is this local counselor I can see, if I wish, just to check upon occasionally. It is not compulsory, as I am not out on any condition. It is simply to receive help here on the outside. I do not have a family, you know, I fell out with them. I have really nowhere to go, so I need to find out what to do with myself."

Michael took another fork and proceeded devouring it all. He enjoyed the meal, so he did not want to rush. He learned to eat slowly, very slowly over the years. Once food arrived, he had nothing else to do but to simply stretch time eating, making the duration of the meal last. There was no other distraction for him.

"Michael don't rush yourself. You can stay here as long as you like. I am also happy to have company. You are my friend. We've known each other for twenty-six years, a long time, so let's stick together, at least for another while. I will show you around and I will be there for you. Now that I am retired, thirty-six years of service, I also do not have any commitments, truly little to do."

"I really do not want to cause any trouble, but thanks, really thanks, I do not know what to say. And this food is delicious, wow, lovely."

"That's okay, you are welcome," Jack chuckled and watched with joy as Michael took another bite.

"So, you have thirty-six years of service then, that is a lot. When did you start working?"

"Well, I finished school and I started at the age of eighteen. I was born in 1968, so I am about three years older than you."

Jack finished his plate first and watched his guest eating slowly, enjoying his meal. He put down his fork and knife, leaned on his elbows and eyed him carefully. Jack waited for a moment and then shot a question at Michael which was completely unexpected. "How about rolling up the case?"

There was a moment of silence and Michael looked up thoughtfully, stunned and startled at the question. "I am not sure I understand. What do you mean?"

"Your case, Michael."

Michael stopped chewing and blinked while looking expectantly at Jack. Then he cut another bite of his toast and put it in his mouth, waiting for Jack to continue. He did not have to wait long.

"Well, you told me many times what happened that night, that you didn't do it, that it was someone else. That there was this guy who was running, and they never identified him."

"Yeah, but after twenty-six years, what am I supposed to do?" he replied, baffled.

Jack twitched his mouth. "There is a lot one can do, even after such time, you'd be surprised. Remember, I was a police officer for about ten years, as you know, before I got transferred as a guard. I know a lot of things, and I can help you."

"Hmm. I don't know."

"What have you got to lose? Or in other words, got any other real plans what to do?"

"What makes you so interested in the case?"

"It is a riveting story, isn't it? I have read so many books about people being imprisoned unfairly and unjustly. When you are a guard at night, you have so little to do. So, I read. The quietness allows you to do so. Any strange noise you realize instantly, so I am able to keep watch while also making time pass by reading and pondering. Well, I also took a great interest in your case and spent hours reviewing it. A lot of it is public, some of it I was able to get access to through my connections in the police force. I have even read the whole transcript of the complete trial, more than once."

Michael nodded and kept chewing slowly on the rest of his toast and scrambled eggs. He really enjoyed every bite. His avocado was long gone. It was probably the most delicious thing he had ever eaten. Most of his food in prison had never been more than simple and tepid, and certainly less tasteful than this meal.

Jack leaned closer. "I believe it was a sordid move by the judge." He twitched his mouth again and took a sip of water while eyeing Michael closely above the rim of the glass. He knew he had touched a raw nerve.

"You mean the judge did not act as he should have?"

"Exactly, unfair, foul play. He just simply dismissed the fact that there was probably someone else also on the scene. There was a witness who said that she saw someone else running. But it was not pursued further. Did you notice how the judge so quickly dismissed the idea and tried to move on to other evidence?"

"It was a long time ago; you remember all this?"

"I was not at the trial, but as I said, I read the transcript, in detail. It's all there. If you want, I can give it to you to scan through. I have a copy here."

"I will think about it. It is not really something I fancy reading, after getting out. I'd rather forget what had happened."

"Do you know how many times I've been to the crime scene?"

"I guess a couple of times?"

"Not once. Except, except of course the one time I was on the case, the following day."

A moment of silence followed. Michael finished his last fork, took a paper napkin, and wiped his mouth. Jack kept watching him intensely. "Going back to that place is not what I had planned, certainly not on my own volition."

Jack sat back. "Think about it. You got nothing to lose. Just go there and see. We can go to the bar and have a drink there, the one you left that night." Jack's eyes were sparkling, while Michael frowned. He continued, "We go to the bar, have a drink, replay what happened. You may remember things you hadn't before. You haven't been there since you were taken away in that police car. They never replayed the event. I'm telling you, the way the trial went was not how it should have."

"Okay, if you insist, we can do so."

"Attaboy. Let me clear up. Want to watch some television, take a nap, or go for a stroll outside? I suggest we go this evening to the bar, once it is dark. Replays the scene better. I'll pay, don't worry."

Michael exhaled and nodded. "Okay, your call. I am your guest here."

CHAPTER 8

The Crime Scene

They spent the afternoon locally, strolling around, while Jack continued to amaze Michael with all the updates of the era. The different events over the last years, news about sports, politics, all which was hidden from him. As Michael had never had any visitors, he knew little of what went on outside of the prison walls. When evening approached, they set off in the car towards the center of town, where Jack parked. Michael watched again with fascination how the vehicle self-maneuvered into a tiny space between two other cars. They got out and started walking towards the bar where Michael met up with his friends, twenty-six years ago.

The bar had been called The Duke at that time. They kept part of its original name. They just renamed it The Grand Duke. Michael wondered why as he led the way inside. Jack followed, seemingly all excited to be retracing all the steps that he took once upon a time. As they entered, he realized that everything had changed. It was modernized from a simple bar to a nice dine-in. Three small tables for two were placed along the front window. The counter was refurbished with honey colored walnut and matching highchairs, running all the way around. A lovely smell came from the kitchen. The adjacent pool room had been converted to a dining place, fitted with further tables and seats.

"Looks like someone really cleaned up here, Jack. Used to be a smoky bar. Really pretty."

"Do you know that you're not allowed to smoke anymore inside?"

53

"No, where does it say so? Not that I mind."

"Oh, it was just one of the new laws that was finally passed, actually some time back. It is all about preventing people from exposure to second-hand smoking. Initially the owners of restaurants worried that such laws would harm their business, but now everyone has gotten used it. You just go outside to smoke. Mind you, they are speaking about banning that, too."

"It does actually ring a bell. They discussed it a lot, I remember. There had been considerable amounts of debates I recall, but I had not been there when it was finally forbidden. Wow, so they really did ban smoking inside!"

As Michael and Jack were chatting, a waiter came from the adjacent room. "Your name please, have you reserved?" He offered them a place at an empty table for two, just by the window. As they made themselves comfortable, Michael looked up and saw a blackboard hanging behind the counter with the title *Specials of the day*, written in white chalk across the top. All sorts of dishes were written in an artistic calligraphy. *Penne ai funghi*. Michael recalled this one. It was pasta with mushrooms. Jack took out his smartphone and scanned something square containing black shapes on a white background. Michael stopped reading the specials and craned his neck to see what Jack was doing.

"Here you are Michael, here is the menu. Just scan this code and it comes up on my phone. Something they also invented not long ago."

"Why, are there no menus anymore on paper or in these nice leather-bound books?"

"Ever heard of COVID?"

"What's that?"

Jack blew up his cheeks. "Never mind, Michael."

He decided that he may tell him later. Some people were still wandering around with masks. But as Michael did not ask, he really had no desire to dwell on this subject anymore. With COVID now basically over, many bars now found it very modern not to reintroduce the traditional menus again, which had been banned for hygiene reasons during the hype of the pandemic era. One restaurant owner also realized something very particular. He noticed that his waiters spent too much time at the tables, watching guests make up their mind what they wanted to eat. He therefore introduced the reservation of tables online, and immediately his guests got a link to study the menu. Even a preorder was possible with a click. As less time was wasted by clients studying what they wanted to eat, it reduced the stay-time in his restaurant. As he had a limited seating space, it increased his turnover of clients. Other restaurant operators liked and copied the idea, so it became widespread practice, at least in the town where Jack was living. So, Jack had reserved online two seats and knew what he was going to order for Michael and himself.

"I took the liberty to peek at the menu this morning on my smartphone, after I reserved a table. I will now order a series of tapas, so you can try out what you like."

"Sounds great, I trust you."

"You have many choices here. Either you pick a menu from up there, but the specialty in this place is international tapas. So many little plates, of various dishes, to try out what you like. I guess they must have a great chef in there, to be able to make all these different plates."

"Sure, whatever." Michael simply enjoyed the moment. A new life began for him.

As soon as they had settled, the waiter was already there with his tablet. Jack ordered two different salads, two sorts of grilled meat, olives, dried tomatoes, and for dessert a plate of fresh cuts of pineapple, to share. To drink, still water.

As the waiter listened and plucked away with a plastic pen, Michael watched him curiously and asked, "I came here a long time ago. This restaurant has changed quite a bit, it is really unrecognizable."

"Yes, I bought it just a few years back and did some renovation. Do you like it?"

"Yes, it is very pretty. I see you also changed the name. Why The Grand Duke? It used to be called just The Duke?"

"Oh, it is a play of words," the waiter responded, in an accent that Michael did not recognize. "I come from Luxembourg." Michael raised his eyebrows and wondered where that was. "Did you know we have a Grand Duke? There is only one in this world. There are many Dukes, but only one Grand Duke, and he lives in Luxembourg." The waiter smiled and left.

Michael eyed Jack. "What did he mean?"

Jack shrugged, "Beats me."

Another waiter arrived almost at once and brought a big bottle of water and two glasses. Jack poured two generous measures, took a big swig and Michael followed suit. He thought for a while as he watched the pedestrians on the sidewalk passing by.

"So how do you want to go about this, Jack?"

Jack folded his hands together on the table and fixed Michael with his blue eyes, leaning forward. "We eat, pretend to drink and go when it is dark. We take the way you went that night and will try to unlock that thing in your memory, that something that is hidden."

"Jack, I have been trying this for the past twenty-six years. What is there to unlock?"

"We just need to find the right key, find that little hole somewhere in your brain and turn. You simply have not found the right opener yet."

"I tried them all, the whole bunch, believe me, more than once. I had long enough to check them all."

"Look, we need to go about this methodically and find out what we can, no matter how trivial it may be. It will be cumbersome, but you will be surprised at what can still be dug up after years gone by. Let us go step by step, we are in no hurry."

Michael looked at Jack unconvinced, "If you say so."

Jack took another gulp of his water and smacked his lips out of pleasure, as if he'd had a taste of his favorite cocktail.

"Then it is settled. Let us go out this evening and start to explore. I have a strong intuition that this will mark the beginning of a successful review of the case."

Michael nodded, dubiously. "If you say so."

"Michael be positive, as I said, I have studied your case, I know pretty much everything about it, and I think there is something foul."

"Well, *I* certainly know there is, but why are *you* so convinced?"

"First of all, something is amiss about the sentence. Never asked yourself why you got so long and why you ended up in that prison?"

"Sure, I did, many times, in fact every single day, hour and minute of my first years locked away, until I got bored of thinking about it. If you ponder on something too long, you lose interest. I never got an answer, though. I did have a friend in the first years of my stay, you must remember him, Tom Bane, the chess player and lawyer. He told me the same thing."

Jack put on another of his goofy grins. "Of course, I do, good old Tom, I remember him. You recall, I gave you the chess set after he left." Jack smiled, proudly.

"Thanks again for that. I haven't been able to show my gratitude yet."

"No worries, small gift, I hope it helped you pass time a bit. Anyway, back to Tom. I wondered how he has been coping over recent years. I know he works locally. I tell you what, we can go and find him as well, he will be surely happy to see you. I was on good terms with him too, but I better not meet up personally. He may have a grudge against me. You never know, what they whispered behind my back."

"Yeah, we can do so. Tom was a nice guy; he helped me … somehow. He was also quite perplexed how my case was handled in court and why I had arrived in this particular prison."

Jack eyed him curiously. "Interesting, what else did he say?"

"Look, it was a long time ago, but that part of the conversation we had on his last day and also about someone higher keeping an eye on me, I remember well. He wanted to do some *digging*. Never heard from him again, though, he disappeared."

Jack leaned back and seemed to ponder, looking out of the window for a while. Michael watched him and hadn't seen Jack so silent all day. He cleared his throat but kept quiet. He was not particularly convinced to rework the whole case again. He preferred to just let it go and get on with the remaining part of his life. After all, he could not turn back the hands of time. What would he really gain? It was a question he had posed himself the moment Jack had started the process of relooking at all the aspects of his case.

The plates soon came one after the other with a five-to-ten-minute delay. Once one dish was finished, the next arrived. Michael enjoyed every moment, the crispy salad, garlic stuffed olives and especially the different grilled meats. He did not remember having ever eaten so well. It certainly rivalled the home cooking of Jack.

He had no desire for alcohol when Jack offered. "Better to keep a clear mind. After absenteeism for years, I do not want to risk it."

Jack chuckled at his comment.

It was well after dusk when they left The Grand Duke. Michael was extremely satisfied and thanked Jack for taking the bill. He had money, but it would likely not last forever, as right now he had no income. His account had been frozen when he got incarcerated. Thanks to his once–upon–a–time generous father, he had no student loans, so no financial obligations remained. Therefore, all the money he had sat there during his full sentence, plus interest. At the time of his arrest, he had a savings account with a favorable rate. The bank had the obligation to keep this rate for the duration of his stay. So, the money grew. Other earnings he received by working in prison were transferred weekly to a prison trust account. His frugal life during the twenty-six years, not smoking and spending little, ensured him a nice sum at the end of his stay. The day he was released, the trust account money was sent to his old account, which got reactivated, and to which he gained full access, the day he was set free.

When they left the small restaurant, it was cold. They both buttoned up.

"Which way, Michael? Did you turn right here and then later left, or the other way round?"

"Here, left. I remember it well. See the church there? Always went that way."

They started trotting along, Jack all excited. His companion a bit less. They continued marching, Jack reducing his pace.

"Okay Michael, let us not precipitate this. Slow down and imagine this is the night of that time. You go along and walk. Go to the church, try to retrace your exact steps, and think what happened at any moment."

"Fine, I mean I went that way to the church and then I turned right. But up to that point nothing really happened."

"Go slowly and try to recollect in your mind what occurred."

Michael shrugged his shoulder and continued walking at a slower pace. They went in the direction of the church with its large windows, its walls decorated with small unrecognizable sculptures due to the poorly lit street. When they then turned right Michael hesitated, as he entered the next road. The street was empty, and their footsteps echoed. He had a small flashback of that very evening and his memory brought him back again to that moment of the past. It had been cold and dark, the same obscurity that reigned now. He remembered not feeling too well due to the excess of alcohol. It was all very blurred. He had a lot to drink, and his head was spinning. It had also likely been due to the fact that he had too little to eat that evening, usually then he got drunk quite easily on an empty stomach. It was a bad habit from university times. Lots of work and little time to cook. The quick sandwich did the trick. Different memories of past times and also fragmented ones of that very fatal evening came back to him while they continued striding at a slow pace, Jack following just behind.

Eventually he stopped. "Here, more or less, it must have happened. I remember the series of ventilation shafts from the shops—there had been several homeless people lying on them, to warm themselves." Michael took a few more steps, scanning the area left to right. Just before a small side street to the left he stopped dead. "Right on this spot it must have been. He was lying here."

Jack slowed down to a standstill, pointing to the ground. He turned around and looked in different directions. "You are sure it was here?"

"Yes, sure, from that alley here came Eileen." Michael pointed to the left. "She did not take our route we just took. I remember the large map they displayed during the trial process, with the crime scene, the bars, and the church. She indicated the way she came from the bar she worked, and I had to do the same, to give a description how I arrived here." Jack stood still and listened attentively. "Any thoughts, Jack?"

"Well, basically you came here the way we just did, and Eileen was coming from the alley over here to the left, and the person running from the scene, of course, darted down the same alley in the direction from which Eileen came."

"Yes. And up here somewhere was the other witness that saw me from his window while letting down his blinds." Michael looked up and scanned around. "I think somewhere up there," pointing to a four-story building on the other side of the street.

"So, you arrived, and that witness saw you. But he did not see the person who stabbed Flynn. He must have just appeared the very moment at his window, when you were attending Flynn, basically just as the real killer had already left."

"Yes, Vincent kept on asking him more than once which exact moment of time he saw me. This witness was already quite old, but he had perfect eyesight, he said. He did not wear his reading glasses and was about to go to bed letting down the blinds. Just during this second, he saw me leaning over the body. Bloody hell, couldn't he have gone to bed a minute earlier?"

"Well, I guess it is no use asking him anymore, I doubt he is still alive. He was eighty, I read that in the report."

"If you say so. I do not remember him well. I just recall that he had a thick wooden walking stick when entering the witness stand."

"So, after this old guy saw you, Eileen must have then arrived shortly after."

"Well, yes. She came and just stood there as I checked upon Flynn. And then, already, the sirens of the police car could be heard. This old guy had at once called the cops."

"What is the name of the bar Eileen was working at?"

"It is a pretty weird name. You cannot forget this one: Dry Throat."

"Well, I suppose that name really doesn't wash down so easily and sticks nicely. So where is this Dry Throat? Let us walk up that way, to find that bar, but first think. Let us go back a bit in time. You saw the body and what happened then?"

"I must have seen the person lying here. His back was turned towards me, and I checked up on him."

"Just try to think and bring back your memory. What did you do exactly?"

Michael shook his head, blinked, and closed his eyes. He had a vague vision, which reappeared in some of his dreams. Him approaching a body in a dark passage, kneeling down, and then touching the figure. At this point, he always woke up. It was there where his dream always ended, every time, with him sitting upright in his bed, panting and sweating. He looked at Jack, opened his eyes, stepped forward and knelt. Only this time he was awake. He imagined someone lying there but could not overcome the fact that he was just staring at an empty space.

"Any memories coming back? What did you do?"

"I really do not remember, Jack. I probably tried to turn him round, grabbing him from the front. He was definitely not facing me. I just saw his back. So as there was this knife, protruding from his abdomen, I must have grabbed it with my right hand and with my left I pulled his right shoulder." He stood up and looked down at the empty space on the pavement.

"You said he was still breathing, when you turned him around."

"Yes, that I was sure of. I first assumed he was some homeless guy and wondered what he was doing here in the middle of the walkway."

"And then, you turned him."

"Yes, then I turned him." He breathed in deeply, feeling the fresh air cool his lungs. Then the horrible memories of the trial returned again, how he desperately tried to explain to everyone that he'd only found the body and had wanted to help. He blinked and looked at the empty space on the ground, feeling an icy shiver running down his back.

"Jack, I recall that there was this expert witness, one that Vincent had hired. He had this theory that the person had been still alive, and that the turning had likely displaced the knife and then killed him."

"That's right, Michael. Dr. Brenden was his name. It is written in the protocol, that there were two movements of the knife. First the initial stabbing and then a jerking upwards. I read and reread it several times. His expertise was quite favorable to you. His analysis was that the victim fell after he was stabbed for the first time. Then you found him and turned him, thrusting the knife up through his diaphragm, only accidentally though."

"So, I actually did kill him."

"Look, let's not go that far. The report said, as per medical analysis by Dr. Brenden, that the initial position of the knife, when first being pushed into the body, and the position of the knife after turning were not the same. That is true. But whether the turning was the effect or if he would have died anyway, is not proven. He may not have survived after the first entry of the knife, since he had lost a tremendous amount of blood, as the knife had been rammed upwards into the abdomen. You were certain that he was groaning when you found him, which makes perfect sense. His diaphragm hadn't been pierced at that particular moment, otherwise he would have *gasped for air* and not groaned. Your action was therefore only the second movement."

Michael looked at Jack, bewildered, as if he were an expert in medicine, and nodded, while looking at him a bit relieved. "It does makes sense. I just do not understand why that theory was not held upright in court."

"Evidence, evidence, evidence, they use it to their advantage as they wish."

Michael recalled the expert witnesses giving their theories of what might have happened and the consequential cross examination by the defense and the prosecution. "The prosecution had a different theory, Jack."

"Yes," Jack interrupted. "You took the knife, pushed it in the first time and then pushed it further in a second move."

"I cannot remember his name."

"It was Dr. Pearson," Jack chipped in. "He basically gave his version of the events, as if he was trying to convince the jury that it was just you."

"I remember him, he was indeed quite confident and very accurate in his account."

"Frank Wells, the prosecutor, was renowned to get the best expert witnesses. He paid any price just to get the right statements, believe me. It was all well-rehearsed. They spent hours in the hotel the previous night going over all the statements that had to be made the following day. I know how this works. Ever read John Grisham?"

"Of course, what do you think? We had several of his books in the library. I read and loved all of his novels."

"Well, then you know it all."

Michael wondered how Jack had all the names of the expert witnesses on the tip of his tongue. He shook his head, still trying to make sense of all the discussions and theories held during the trial proceedings. He also replayed them multiple times during his long sentence. However, with the years he got tired of repassing the whole case again in his head. *What is the point anyway?* he asked himself. *It will not change a thing.* But the more he replayed all the scenes, the more he asked himself what he or Vincent could have done differently to convince the jury.

"It is useless what we are doing here, Jack. What difference does it make?"

"Cheer up, young chap, let us go up this way now, and see from where Eileen came. Take it as a personal challenge, what is there to lose?"

Michael was not convinced and felt that Jack was putting him under too much pressure and was about to trot off, following his friend. Before they turned, though, into the road to the left from which Eileen came, Jack stopped and looked straight ahead. "Down there is the casino, about ten minutes from here. From there Flynn Meier came that night."

"So, from that direction ahead came Flynn, from the left here came Eileen and from here, behind, I came."

"Yep, that is how it was."

They both turned left and strolled along, away from the area where Flynn Meier was stabbed. Michael glanced back again a few times and followed Jack. He had a vivid vision of the scene. Him and the body and what had happened. He cursed his clumsiness. "Hell, why can't I remember more?" he said to his partner, frustrated. Then he suddenly stopped and looked down.

"Jack, do you see this?"

"What is it, Michael?"

"This alley is paved with cobblestones."

"So?"

"Well, who would jog this way?"

"That is a good observation. Nobody really wants to twist his ankle. The only question is if it has always been like this."

"I really do not remember, that is clear. Perhaps something to find out by asking some locals here or the commune."

Jack nodded at the comment, and they continued.

"Over there, Michael, more or less is where Eileen reported to have seen this person running."

They were not far away from the scene, in a dark alley, with little light. They continued to walk and came to another junction. Looking left and then right, they saw a few houses in the distance, one of them very brightly lit.

"Doesn't look like an ordinary residence—let's go that way," Jack said, leading the way.

Michael followed behind, his mind somewhere else, reconstructing what he could remember.

Eventually they approached the bright light and when they stood in front of it, they faced a large window with the black letters 'Dry Throat' across.

"Well, she didn't go far before she saw that person, unfortunately she could not give a good description of him." Jack looked across to see Michael's reaction.

Michael just stood there, contemplating. "Why does it have to be a man. Could have been a woman, no?"

Jack nodded, "Perhaps. But normally you can tell by the gait if it is a woman or man."

"I cannot remember if this question was posed."

"One more reason to see the witness, Eileen. We will find out where she lives," Jack grinned and slapped Michael sideways on the shoulder. "With her full name we can get her address. It is quite easy nowadays to get hold of someone when you know their name."

Michael nodded silently, with his hands trembling slightly in his pocket. He was shivering; however, not from the cold but from reliving his trauma of the past. He had suffered often from post-traumatic stress over recent years. The trial, the terrible events of the conviction, and then the incarceration were stored deep inside his body. They were locked away and were then suddenly released at any moment arousing depression, anxieties, and even heart palpitations. He had learned that deep long breaths and thinking positively helped him to overcome these difficult moments. Being with Jack and having someone to speak to did help. The situation of digging up a difficult past, though, was awfully hard and very counterproductive.

"Are you okay, Michael, anything wrong?" Jack noticed that Michael was shaking slightly and steadied him, putting a friendly hand on his shoulder.

Michael closed his eyes, inhaled, and then exhaled slowly, trying to steady himself. "I am fine, thanks. I am still suffering from past events and my body behaves funny at times."

"Take it easy, let's walk back to the car and then go home, it's been a long day."

Michael smiled again, taking deep breaths. He realized that the loss of memory of the very night when he saw Flynn Meier lying in the street preoccupied him most, though. What had really happened was not clear to him. Over the years he tried many times to recollect those crucial moments, but they were simply wiped away. If only he could remember more and why he moved the body. Perhaps it was his state of inebriation at that time that caused this loss of memory. He swore never to touch alcohol again in his life.

CHAPTER 9

The Witness

When they got home, Michael felt better after closing his eyes for a while in the car. They settled on the couch and Jack zapped through the TV channels to show his guest the news of the recent era, new films, and innovations. Everything appeared so different to the time when he last watched; so much had changed. As interesting as it all was, Michael felt a sense of instability and anxiety. He was stranded in a new world, completely helpless and was asked to now survive. It was like arriving at an unknown place on earth with just a small bag and nowhere to go, alone, powerless, and under pressure. He still carried the stigma of a criminal, someone who had served time, viewed as if he were a villain, looked down upon. His innocence did not have any weight. So many concerns, so many worries were circulating in his head.

When Michael finally retired for the night, he lay there with his eyes open. Every sound was new. The smell was different, and the bed, unquestionably, provided a newfound level of comfort. He was afraid to close his eyes. He feared waking up and opening them to find himself in prison once more, so great was his anxiety. His quest for freedom had grown so big that the fear of not gaining it had equally developed inside. "Relax, this is real. I am out," he whispered to himself while he heard Jack snoring away on the sofa. He gazed into the darkness and wondered what the future held for him.

He finally shut his eyes and fell into a deep dream, wandering back to his prison cell. He was there on his bed and was waiting for Jack to open the observation window. He saw the moonlight and was speaking to the man on the moon. Occasionally he woke up, and he did not know where he was, not sure if he was awake or dreaming. His mind had not settled and had not accepted that he was no longer in his cell. It was an uneasy first night waking up several times in agitation and trying to get back to sleep.

It was only with the first sunlight coming from the street, the odd car passing by, and Jack in the shower whistling along, that brought the certainty that he was really here, in another place. It took a moment to remember, but it was where Jack had taken him yesterday. He recognized a bigger room, other furniture, and his cushion was certainly softer. He lay there for a while until there was a knock on the ajar door and Jack peeked in with a radiant look on his face, his cheeks flushed red from the hot shower.

"Good morning young chap! You slept like a log this morning. I have prepared something to start the day. Come along. If you want to have a shower first, go ahead. Then we will check how to find Eileen." Jack disappeared through the doorway.

"Good morning, Jack, I will be along in a moment." Michael looked at the ceiling and was not quite sure how to interpret his feeling of freedom. More than a hint of angst of having to face a new life was stuck somewhere deep inside of him. The realization of the momentous task ahead came crushing down. He had not expected that this burden could outweigh the joy of freedom. He shut his eyes for a few moments and took long deep breaths, before heading for the bathroom.

They ate breakfast and Michael relished his freshly brewed breakfast coffee for the first time in many years. Milk and cereals were tasty; he could not remember such a wonderful early morning meal. While his anxiety still hung heavy on his body, he tried to relax and to just enjoy the moment and the companionship. Instead of eating in solitude, there was somebody with him.

After clearing up, Jack switched on his computer, making himself comfortable on his swivel chair. Michael was standing behind him, admiring his skills. After just a few clicks he was excited.

"There she lives. Look, Eileen Parker. Her address is Winston Road 194. Easy-peasy."

"Pretty amazing this computer, I have to say. So fast and also the images are so clear."

"This is a high-resolution screen. Good for watching videos on the Internet. Nowadays, you can see anything you like, from old pop-videos to recent films. You can even watch live sports events. Just sign up with some streamer and you are in."

"Sure," Michael responded, skating over the exact truth that he had actually not understood a thing.

"Nowadays it is easy to track down anybody. With all the social media, you cannot imagine how people share insight even to their private life."

"What is social media?"

"Huh, yeah. You probably had e-mail when you were at university?"

"Yeah, I did."

"Right, this is a bit of an extended version if you'd like to see it this way. Look, there are many ways to communicate nowadays. People use different programs and put all types of information about themselves into these. What they do is to put their photos with friends, photos with family, where they are, holiday snaps, really anything. You can then, if you click on their name, get access to these at any time round the clock, and you can check all the information being put there. There is this modern phrase called *posting*. So, anything a person shares, so called "posts," is public. There are people who post their entire day for the world to follow."

"Interesting."

"Well, people do become careless often, and there is a lot of misuse. Somebody just posts from the seat of the plane that they are off on vacation, and the next moment, somebody says *thank you* and robs his house, because they know there is nobody home. The days of privacy are gone unless you decide to live a life of very low profile."

"Why should I want to share with the world where I am going?"

"Ha, you'd be surprised what people do nowadays. Do you know what a *trend* is?"

"I guess something that is popular, I assume."

"I am impressed, I did not expect this good response. You are absolutely right. It is a trend to inform the world what you do at any moment in life. And believe it or not, people spend hours every day just to follow what other people do and say."

"Wow. How do you digest so much information?"

Jack looked at Michael, quite surprised at the astuteness of his comment. "Our brains are learning to become superficial; we see, hear, look, and then move to the next. The days of thinking about something more profound are gone." After a few clicks, Eileen was up on the screen. "There she is, just looked her up."

Michael regarded her and a serene feeling overcame him. He remembered her well from the trial, even though a long time had passed. Eileen hadn't changed much; still beautiful, like his mother. His memories wandered back to his parents.

"You recognize her?"

She had some wrinkles under her eyes, but her expression was still the same: calm, and honest. "Yes, it is her, I cannot forget her face, her demeanor, even though I only saw her for some sixty minutes at the trial."

"Do you want to see her house where she lives? You can even check that on the Internet as well."

"Nah, it is okay, I need to take this one at a time. My head is already steaming with all this information." Michael kept looking at her, marveling.

"Better get used to it, my friend. Welcome to the new world. These days you are overthrown with everything that happens on this planet; people tell you what they are up to, and you get bombarded with personal messages."

Jack got up and tapped Michael on the shoulder then disappeared into the kitchen, leaving him to continue staring at Eileen. He recalled the faces of his parents, his father and that smile of his mother, after she gave him a kiss on the cheek. *It was nice of you to drop by this weekend. Enjoy your week.* With these words he left them as he hopped onto the bus back to the place where he lived and worked. They waved goodbye as the bus pulled away. Then a final glance into the face of his mum, and that was the last time he had seen her smiling. *So more or less that is how she must look like today, probably,* he thought to himself, as he glanced once more at Eileen, before the screensaver was activated. He turned and joined Jack in the kitchen, where he was peeling onions and squashing garlic.

"I am going to make us a vegetable broth, you will love it. Lots of vitamins for you, it is especially good for this time of year." Jack kept finely chopping celery, carrots, and mushrooms on the worktop and peeked at

Michael. "Let us plan a surprise visit to her tomorrow, or if you are up to it, already this afternoon, what do you say?"

Michael reflected. "Look, Jack, don't get me wrong, but give me another day or so. This is all a bit too much to digest. I've only just got out. I have to get used to the taste of normal life again. Plunging myself headfirst into rerunning events of a bad past is not what I wanted to do. Please, do give me a few more days to adjust."

Jack nodded solemnly. "You're the guest. Let us catch some fresh air now and walk while I let this simmer. I will show you around. I live in a quiet area. The activity will also do you good. You need to get used to a bit of walking and exercise your leg muscles a bit." Jack nodded excitedly after Michael gave him an acknowledging smile. They put on their coats and stepped outside for a stretch.

The walk during the day and also after dusk became a ritual. They strolled all over the city and often exchanged their views on books they read, observed the people, and talked about cooking. Michael was cautious about health. He knew he had lost part of his life and was determined to extend the rest as much as possible. Healthy meals were the best way to achieve this. So, they also discussed recipes and what to prepare the next day. Jack explained that there were all types of programs one could see online and just be guided by someone when cooking. *There is this word again, online,* he reflected, what does that mean again? He understood it was something to do with the computer and this internet.

Most of the time though, they walked without uttering a word. Michael was happy to do so; he was used to it. He just enjoyed the quiet promenades and was simply glad to have company.

When they returned, they settled on the patio, under thick blankets, and listened to the different sounds, like the occasional car passing by or the birds chirping away, communicating among each other; it was spring, and it was time for them to find a companion. Occasionally they opened the odd beer, alcohol-free. Sometimes little was said, but Jack could not resist telling his guest about notable events that occurred over the years. Sports, politics, and finance–Jack gave Michael the full rundown.

As a plane passed overhead, he asked him, "Have you ever flown, Michael? I haven't, I am a bit aerophobic. Did you know, even sport celebrities are sometimes. They just attend home games if the away game is too far away."

"Yes, I have taken the plane. Not much though, ugh, last time it was one Christmas, my dad took me and mum to New York, for shopping. I never understood what is so great about this. Crammed among so many people, finding things you may want to buy, but you do not need. I certainly enjoyed the sightseeing part. It was bitter cold, I recall."

"Beautiful city. I have never been. A lot has changed since 9/11."

"What's that?"

"9/11? Never heard what happened?"

Michael shook his head, taking a sip from his bottle. "Enlighten me."

Jack paused for a moment, as he was unsure what to say, but then tried to formulate his response carefully: "There were these people who had decided to take control of some planes and two of them were flown into the Twin Towers. It all burned down. It was one of the saddest moments of everyone's lives. I cannot remember how many, but several thousand innocent people lost their lives. What a terrible and sad world we live in, Michael."

Incredulously Michael looked at Jack. "You can't be serious!" Michael shook his head in disbelieve. There was a long silence.

Then Michael asked, "And the towers, they are gone?"

"Yes, gone and they erected a new building."

Bewildered, Michael continued to shake his head. He clearly saw the images as he went to New York with his parents. Yes, it was Christmas, he was still at school, in his last year. They took the elevator in the South Tower and at the top there was a huge panorama window. You could walk around and look out in all directions. He recalled seeing the Statue of Liberty, how beautiful she stood there. They sat down on the leather benches for hours, admiring the Big Apple. It was breathtaking. In the elevator back down, he met a smartly dressed lady in her thirties. She was of pure character, honest, smiling, and inspiring. They chatted all the time on the long way descending to the ground floor. Outside they shook hands. *It was lovely making your acquaintance. Here is my business card. I work here in this building. Call me when you are in town next.*

He sat there consternated, pinching his nose, his vision lost far beyond the floorboards. He remembered her so well; the encounter was as if it had occurred yesterday. He wondered what happened to her. *Did she survive?*

He wiped a tear coming from his left eye; it was so shocking for him to hear this.

"I still have the card she gave me. It must be together with the video tapes. I had this handheld Japanese camcorder. Once the cassette recordings were full, I transferred these onto video tapes. This way we could see them on the television using the video recorder. I stuck her card into the case of the tapes."

"We don't use any more of these nowadays. It's all digital." Jack watched him sadly. "Cheer up. A lot of dreadful things have happened over the last years. Humanity hasn't changed."

Michael slept badly again that night, with the images of him and his parents in New York. They went into the Twin Towers, and they shook as they were admiring the city through the large windows. All the people were screaming and were running for the stairs. He called for his mother and could not find her. He saw her sitting solemnly on a chair, looking out. *We need to get out, hurry, hurry,* he screamed. *Why, what is wrong?* his mother answered, quietly. He tried to pull her up and struggled to get her onto her feet. He grabbed her around the waist. *Hurry up, hurry up.* They wanted to take the elevator and his father was already inside, stopping the doors from closing. Desperately he pushed himself towards the lift, his mother moving only slowly, as he tried to pull her along. But his steps were heavy. He could not move, as hard as he struggled. Every step was like sinking into deep snow. The elevator kept on moving away, with the doors closing and his father disappearing behind them. It was so hot that abruptly, Michael awoke.

He sat upright in his bed, feeling the sweat running down his forehead. He looked outside; the moon was shining. He had to collect himself. He was at the home of Jack. He wiped his face with his sleeve and went to the kitchen to get a glass of water. He remained awake until sunrise, his heart still pounding more than usual all morning; a new day to come.

During breakfast, Jack listened to Michael's nightmare attentively. "You have been through much during the past years. All the different events that happened in your absence and your adjustments to the new situation are a lot to take for you. Your brain must sort it accordingly. It is like reading a book about something completely new to you. The difference is simply that you are reading twenty-six years of contemporary history within a few days. This may be a lot to take."

"Let us get on with it then. Perhaps it is time to check upon Eileen. To do nothing may not help, otherwise I ponder too much."

Jack, of course, was all in. "I was already getting impatient," Jack said, mockingly and grinning. They got ready after breakfast and drove off.

"Here, I put the address into the navigation system. Have you ever seen one?"

"I remember the basic models, but not so sophisticated and not with these screens. They're quite astonishing. I still used a map. Got you also from A to B. It was like orienteering during my scouting days."

"You know what the disadvantage is today using these? Nobody has any sense of orientation anymore. Just put the destination into your smartphone and walk. When I was small, I had a compass. Or on vacation, you looked at the city plan and went north or west. You knew where everything was relative to you."

Michael nodded as the young voice told Jack to turn left at the next junction and then after hundred meters, right again.

CHAPTER 10

Eileen

"184, 186, 188, there it is. I will stop here and let you out." Jack came to a halt on the side of the street after checking his mirror and pointed ahead.

"Aren't you coming along?"

"No, I better not. I was not part of the case. Eh, I think it is better you go on your own. She may be too intimidated by two strangers. She never met me either. I think she will speak more freely to you without my presence. Perhaps she still remembers you."

Michael shrugged, lifted the door handle with his right hand and got out. Jack bent down and leaned on the passenger side to be able to look at Michael. "You see that intersection over there in the distance, there where there is an overhead electric line running across? There, I will be waiting for you behind the corner."

"What shall I do if she is not in?"

"We will try again later."

"Okay, Jack, let's see."

He closed the door and watched Jack pull off swiftly in his silent car, then started walking towards 194.

As he approached Eileen's house, he saw a petite lady walking towards him with two shopping bags in her hand. She then turned and entered the gate to house number 194. He accelerated a bit.

"Excuse me, ma'am. Sorry to disturb you, my name is Michael Fletcher."

The lady stopped dead, spun around and eyed him carefully top to bottom, squinting her eyes. After a few seconds she opened them wide. "I know you! Oh my god, you were the one in that court room, poor thing."

"I am very sorry if I startled you."

"Oh, no, I remember you well. I think about you often, still today. I am so sorry for the way they treated you. I still discuss it with my husband often. Really, I can assure you, I never believed you were guilty, I am so sorry. Well, look at you, it is quite remarkable, you haven't changed a bit, you still look so much the same."

"Yeah, I just spent twenty-six years in a wellness center. Sleep, healthy diet, no alcohol, no cigarettes, no stress."

He was surprised at his own comment and caught himself almost smiling. As he looked at her his heart leapt. She was truly a lookalike of his mother. He had the same feeling as when he saw her at court years back. Eileen raised her eyes and smiled broadly at him. She wore a thick leather jacket and had her hair up, tied into a bun. He marveled at her beauty.

"Please do come in, if you just help me with this bag, so I can pick the keys out of my pocket."

She handed Michael one of the shopping bags, took out a set of keys, opened a swinging door followed the next, unlocking it.

"Come in, don't be shy. Let me take that bag off you. I will just hop into the kitchen and will store all this away. Won't be a moment, please sit down, make yourself at home."

Michael stepped into a nicely furnished living room. It was essential, but clean. His nose was tickled by a soft honey perfume, emitted by a bunch of Lily flowers placed neatly in a high glass vase. The place reminded him much of his home. His mother had also often brought in flowers to decorate. He wondered at that moment again what his parents were doing, and if she still kept the same habit of decorating the room.

Eileen came out of the kitchen and saw a distant but serene look on his face and paused briefly before saying in a soft tone, "You must be hungry, I suppose, love. Let me fix you some coffee. This morning I made some muffins. They are yummy and still warm."

Michael smiled as he looked into her face. "I do not want to cause any trouble, Mrs. Parker."

Eileen had already disappeared into the kitchen as he perceived her calling, "Please do call me Eileen."

All sorts of sounds followed from the clinking of plates and cups and then a percolator crackling. He made himself comfortable on the sofa and admired a picture with a thick silver frame, which was placed on the center table. It had Eileen in the middle, smiling broadly, with two men on each side, one younger and the other a bit older. He guessed that they must be her husband and son. Eileen entered soon with a tray holding two cups of coffee, milk, sugar, and a large plate piled with white sugar-coated cakes.

"Here you are, my dear. You must be starving. No modesty, please help yourself. Milk, sugar?"

He got up and settled at the table. "Yes, please, very kind of you."

He picked up a muffin and took a deep bite. He closed his eyes and savored the moment. It was, once more, as if it was one of the most delicious things he had ever tried.

"Good, aren't they! Please help yourself to more, and here is your coffee," which Eileen placed in front of him. "Let me just move the photo to the side, to make some space."

"Is this your family, Eileen?"

"Yes, this is my son, Justin, he is now working up north, as a teacher. He enjoys it very much. All these kids, he phones me every day and keeps on telling me all sorts of stories. Last week, you cannot imagine what happened, one young boy brought this snake into school. Nobody knew, until something touched Justin's feet. He leapt onto the table. All that the kid in the first row did was to get up with a smile, take the snake and put it back into his bag. Yesterday Justin phoned me again. They made it a school rule now that no pets are allowed into the school, prior to the principal's permission."

Michael chuckled. He added some milk and sugar to his coffee, shaking his head while stirring it.

"And this, dear, here is my husband. Lovely chap, we have now been married for almost 30 years. We are both retired, and it is a bit difficult to get by these days. All has become so expensive. You cannot imagine how much you spend nowadays, going shopping. I used to fill four shopping bags with the same money I do today for two bags. Fruits or meat have all become so unaffordable, and it is not that we are getting a higher pension to compensate for all this. So, my husband is actually a part-time Taxi driver, to earn us some extra money. However, he is also complaining, as people have become less generous in tipping. Everyone is so hard done by. You know, I was a waiter in a restaurant, or let's call it more of a bar, but I got a bit too old for the likings of the owner, and now I am looking only after the house."

Eileen sat down opposite him and gave a lovely smile while Michael took another bite of the great-looking muffins. She blew into her cup and eyed her guest, enjoying the moment of company.

Eileen continued speaking, placing down her cup. "You know I stopped working not long ago at this bar, but I still go there sometimes to say hello to a dear friend of mine. It is difficult to let go when you have been there for a great part of your life. It is a part of you. I was there only last week. This bar was the same one that I left that night. Was it really twenty-six years ago? You know, every time I walk back, the terrible event springs to my mind. It is strange you dropped by today. I thought about you, well, yes, a few days ago, when I visited my friend there. This horrible occurrence seemed like yesterday." Eileen took her cup, sipped her coffee carefully and paused to order her thoughts, then said, "That night when I was walking home, when that murder occurred, I mean when this person got stabbed, I finished late. I left and wanted to catch the night bus. That is when I saw this guy running past me."

Michael pushed the last bit into his mouth, swallowed and looked at Eileen intensely. "I recall when you testified, you saw this person. But somehow, the whole thing was dismissed. It was somebody going for a jog."

"Michael, I am sure, as I was also at the time, this guy was not doing any sports. He was acting differently. He literally sprinted, he ran, but in a very uneasy and agitated manner. It was not controlled or relaxed."

"But you did not recognize him."

"I am so sorry; it was dark, but he was definitely about your size and build. Even though this whole event happened so long ago, I just cannot forget it. I still discuss it with my husband today. I simply cannot let go of it."

Michael nodded as he helped himself to the inviting cup of coffee. It was good, particularly good, so he took a few more sips, almost emptying his cup.

Eileen looked at him with a guilty feeling, "I-I am terribly sorry not to have been more precise during the questioning. I did not know how to help you further, but I was sure, as I am still today, that this person whom I saw had something to do with the stabbing, I just felt it. I mean, who runs around so agitatedly in the middle of the night? It was in the early hours of the morning and the alley was not well lit. I was walking down the road towards the bus stop. Then suddenly he dashed right past me. I was actually a bit startled, as I did not see him coming. I did hear some steps approaching, but it all went so fast. If it had been someone regular, going for a jog at night, surely, I would have come across him again."

"How far were you from the scene, when you saw him?"

"The police never really verified the exact distance. But as I walked the same way the following nights, I got a bit of a feeling for the time it took, as all the memories kept coming back. I do not think it was more than a minute, at most."

"So, when you saw the person sprinting past you, you must have arrived at the scene about a minute later."

"I guess, yes."

"And then you saw me."

"Yes, you, as you were leaning over the body," she said, looking at him pitifully.

Michael tilted his head sideways and looked up, trying to reflect. "Unbelievable. It took you a minute to walk to the scene. Of course, it took that runner probably not even half that time from the scene until you saw him; at most ninety seconds had passed. I guess I saw Flynn lying on the ground only seconds after the assassin ran away."

"Yes, likely not much time must have passed. He was lying on his back when I came, and you had already turned him around. So, you must have attended him some time."

Michael peered blankly into the distance, beyond the table, and took the cup between his hands, feeling the warmth between his palms. Another question then jogged his memory.

"Eileen, this passageway–I walked along it again the other day. I realized it is cobblestoned. Has it always been that way?"

"Well, let me think, I have been walking along that way for the last thirty or odd years. I am sure not to have noticed it being different. I certainly do not recall any roadwork, so I guess, indeed, it has always been like this. Why do you ask?"

"I was just wondering. It does not make sense for someone to jog along a cobblestone path. Especially at night, how easy to take a sudden wrong step and you damage your ankle."

"Now that you are mentioning it, true. It certainly was neither brought into consideration during the trial, at least not when I was there."

Michael once more realized how many gaps and unanswered questions there were in the case. The more he thought about it the bigger the pain became again. As his face contorted in anguish, Eileen watched him intensely and wanted to cheer him up. "Do you want another muffin? Or can I get you anything else?"

"No thank you Eileen, you have been too kind, I really appreciate you having invited me here. Thank you. I am fine. My stomach isn't used to eating so much. I need to watch out a bit."

Michael felt himself really smile, probably for the first time in as long he could remember. Eileen returned the smile and blinked. They talked away for at least another hour. Eileen made another cup of coffee and Michael was convinced to enjoy a further cake. She asked him all sorts of questions about his present stay and what he was doing, taking care to avoid anything of the past. She was very considerate and did not want to upset him.

"Remember, you are welcome here at any time. Please come again. I would very much like you to meet my husband; he is in fact very eager to get to know you. You must understand, we speak about you often. I just can't forget what happened. Numerous times we have had this conversation, and my husband keeps telling me not to get too agitated. For me, having sat in that courtroom was not a pleasant experience; it is still haunting me after all these years. And then they accused me of being drunk after one glass - pathetic. They were all so unfriendly and aggressive, not nice at all in that court room."

I bet they weren't, Michael thought to himself, *They did not treat me any differently.* He put down his cup after finishing it. "Thank you, Eileen, thank you, indeed. It was a pleasure to see you. It was truly kind of you to invite me in. I enjoyed being here, believe me, I will come again, I promise."

"No worries, it was a real pleasure to have someone around. Best to try in the afternoons, before four o'clock. That is the least of the busiest times for my husband. Most people are still at work. After five it becomes hectic again for him."

"Okay, will do so, give him my warmest regards, and thank you once more for your kind hospitality."

Eileen waved him off after giving Michael a big hug. He was so taken aback that he just stood there like a dummy, his hands simply dangling down. He wasn't used to the human touch anymore, especially not from somebody of the opposite sex. The peck on the cheek made him blush.

As Michael walked away, he was still overwhelmed by the kindness he had received. His body had just obtained a caring touch, something that had been denied to him for twenty-six years. The last one was when he had said goodbye to his parents, that weekend he visited them for the very last time.

He headed for the next junction and found Jack sitting in his car with his eyes closed. The passenger door was locked, so he knocked on the window. Jack jolted, lowered his head to see who was there, smiled, rubbing one eye, and pushed a button, unlocking the central system. Expectantly he watched as Michael got in, starting the car.

"So, tell me all. What happened?"

"Not much really, Eileen was truly kind. I had lots to eat and some great coffee."

"What did she say?"

"Well, she confirmed to me once more that she saw this guy but could not recognize him. Something she had already said during the trial. But she did tell me also that she was very sure that this person seemed suspicious. He was somewhat very uncontrolled and agitated, not like a regular jogger, dashing past her."

"You see, it confirms our theory. We are making progress."

"If you say so."

"Evidence, evidence, evidence. We need to take one step at a time, collect the facts and use them systematically. By the way, did you ask her if she thinks it may have been a woman?"

"No, I missed that point. I may have to go back. I promised her anyway to return."

"Okay, that is fine, let us remember this for next time. I propose that we will now try to find your old attorney."

"Pfff, I really do not want to see him. Vincent disillusioned me. He could have done more."

"Maybe yes, but let's find out more about what happened. Let's kick ass. There must have been a reason why he was so reluctant to fight for you."

"You want me to become aggressive?"

"Nah, don't worry, but a little pressure won't harm, will it?"

He wondered what Jack meant. He certainly wanted to stay out of trouble. "I hope we are doing the right thing."

"We cannot change the past, but we will try to adjust the future. How does that sound?"

Michael nodded, unconvinced. They headed home and then took another stroll to clear their minds. In the evening Jack took the rest of the vegetable broth he had prepared the day before and added some shredded chicken and Chinese noodles. Then he let it simmer, adding a couple drops of soy sauce. Michael enjoyed every spoon and thanked Jack again for his care.

After dinner, Jack typed away once more on his personal computer and swiftly found all the details of his ex-lawyer, Vincent Graham. Michael sat next to him, watching and learning how to use the modern operating systems.

"Look here Michael, he must be retired. His resumé is listed here and stops a few years back. He seems to still offer personal consultations though. His profile is still listed as an active lawyer. And here further below, voilà, we have his address. He is still living in town. I know this place. It is not too far from here, maybe thirty minutes at most. Let's go the first thing tomorrow morning, for an early start. It would be advisable to go unannounced."

"Why is that?"

"Better to catch him off guard. He has some explaining to do and cannot avoid you if you simply present yourself. Also, if we are early enough, he is more likely to be in."

"Okay then. I wake up early anyway."

Michael slept a bit better that night; however, he still woke up occasionally and then went back to sleep, gliding between dreams and reality. He was, luckily, in great physical condition, which helped. In prison he hadn't worked hard, had eaten moderately and well, and had abstained from any drugs or cigarettes. His sleeping rhythm had improved greatly over the last years, with a healthy, undisturbed eight to nine hours. He had absolutely no sleep deprivation. He was simply in perfect shape. The only thing he had to control was his mental state. It suffered greatly, especially in the first years. With time though, he worked on controlling his anguish by taking deep breaths and exhaling slowly, calming himself down. It was a method he had read about in one of the books, *Speaking about Yoga*. By controlled breathing he managed to reduce his agitation and unrest. This way he was especially able to control the fear he had at times, not being able to cope with his new life and surroundings.

CHAPTER 11

Vincent

The following morning, after a quick orange juice, coffee, and toast, they set off early to see Vincent. The traffic was still light and they arrived at eight o'clock sharp, before the morning rush, at a modern riverside residence consisting of two glass-facade eight-story towers. Michael debated briefly whether it was too early to present himself unexpectedly at this hour, but Jack assured him, better now than not to find him home later.

"Be nice, but ensure you show yourself disappointed. After all, he was your lawyer and when they locked you up, he deserted you. Find out why."

Jack insisted on the same procedure; he preferred not to be part of the visit and sent Michael alone to the big tower. He found the name *Vincent Graham* on a push-button panel with numbers from zero to eight, among a long list of names, and was a bit confused as to what to do. There were only numbers to push. He then quickly figured out that he had to push eight and then two. Eighth floor, apartment two. He pushed the numbers one after the other and waited.

"Top floor, the elevator is coming down," someone echoed through the speaker.

There was a click and a buzz, and the front door unlocked. He stepped inside and took an elevator that appeared and opened. There were no buttons. The door shut automatically and he moved up. Shortly after, it reopened, and he saw Vincent standing in front of him.

"Oh, who are you? I expected someone else."

"You do not recognize me, do you?"

Vincent looked hard and opened his eyes wide. A few seconds passed. "Oh, shit, it's you, Michael Fletcher, what are you doing here?"

"Come to see you."

"What for?"

"To talk."

"Look, I only have a few minutes, sorry, I am expecting someone else. Please do come in."

He turned and led the way from the elevator corridor into a modern apartment overlooking the city. "Have a seat."

Several bean bags and low tables were spread around. But when Vincent pointed to the highchairs at the kitchen bar, Michael was relieved. He never liked these bags when he was younger, as they became more popular. In fact, their original name, *Sacco,* came from an Italian designer, and it means sack. Well, that is what he felt like sitting in them—in a saggy sack, disappearing.

Vincent was only a bit older than him but had aged much more in a hardworking world. Lawyers often worked in big firms with long hours; he had probably been no exception. Michael did not really care what his ex-attorney had done in life but was much more intrigued why he had not heard from him since he had been locked away. No call, no visit, not even a letter. Vincent sat down next to him after turning his chair to face him, tucking in his shirt and buttoning it up. His host made no sign of offering a welcome coffee. He assumed that Vincent would at least greet him with a handshake and a drink; after all, he was his ex-client. But instead, an uninterested nod was offered. His hair was still slicked back as Michael remembered him, just grey.

"Thank you for seeing me." Michael intended to remain polite, to stay objective and not to become too aggressive, as hard as it would be. He knew he would not achieve anything otherwise. He had discussed with Jack at length how to go about the conversation. *First try to collect evidence, which is the first step.*

Michael detected a hint of nervousness as Vincent settled. His lawyer was clearly uncomfortable with the situation. He recalled a different demeanor;

back then, Vincent appeared decidedly less agitated. A silence hung in the room and grew. Michael felt that Vincent did by no means want to start the conversation, so he simply asked casually, but with a clear aim behind his question. "Are you still practicing or are you retired?"

"Is this just an opening for small talk? Otherwise, I do not understand your question. This is not why you came here, I suppose."

"Well, I want to know if you retired and when. I do not recollect having ever heard from you again after the trial, basically after I was put away." Michael let the sentence settle before he decided to go for the final punch. "So, if you retired, did you retire twenty-six years ago?"

"I think you are being a bit sarcastic here."

"Not really. You were my lawyer, I was found guilty, it was your job to appeal, to shorten the sentence, do whatever to help me. But you simply disappeared, and I was left alone." Michael was suddenly feeling frisky, playful, and full of energy. He wanted answers he had never received.

"Look, let me start. After the verdict I made an appeal for your case to be reviewed …"

"Reviewed, what does that mean? I had never, ever seen or heard anything from you, neither of any kind of action or appeal to try to help me. It was as if you had just forgotten about me—there was nothing but absolute silence. You let me sit there with no help, no message, nothing."

"I did not come to see you, that's right, but I did send you, if I recall well, three letters."

"Never got them. What letters?"

"Well, sorry, I sent them, addressed to you."

"What was in them?"

"That I was working on the appeal, which was my first letter. Years later I also sent you another two letters. I wrote that you should try to present yourself in front of a parole board, to ask for an early release."

Well, I figured that out myself actually, Michael thought, but refrained from saying. "I did, but with little success. The petition was rejected, not just once but three times."

"I do not know what to say, Michael. I tried and I wrote to you. But you must also understand that the case was taken away from me directly after I sent you that first letter mentioning the appeal. I was assigned elsewhere. Even then I had not forgotten you. Therefore, I sent the other two as I learned you were still in prison, years later. A visit, though, was not possible. I did not represent you anymore."

"The case was taken away from you and assigned elsewhere, oh yeah? To whom was it assigned?"

"I was not told."

"And who assigned you elsewhere?"

"No idea. I worked at the time for the public sector. I got a correspondence and was asked to handle another case. I was under the impression that your case was really transferred."

"That's cheap. You got another assignment, and I was history."

"As I said, I tried and was not on your case anymore, but I had not forgotten you. This is all I can say."

"You make it sound all amazingly simple, fait accompli, is it? Now I come and see you after such a long time and you have nothing else to say."

"Look, Michael, sorry to seem rude, I simply did not expect you this morning. This is more than a surprise visit, you must understand. It was good to see you again and I'm glad you're out. But I need to really get going. I have more pressing matters at hand."

Michael had no desire to end the conversation right now. "The trial did not go as it should have, especially the part where the witness, Eileen Parker, was so easily dismissed."

"Michael, this was an awfully long time ago. What are you trying to achieve now?"

"I want answers and you owe me these. Too many gaps and unanswered questions I have been fighting with over the many years. Do you know what that means?"

Vincent looked at his ex-client with some compassion and recalled the witness he had brought to testify. "Yes, I remember her well. Unfortunately, she was discredited by the prosecution."

"She was sure that there was another person running from the scene. I even saw her yesterday and she recalls well the mysterious runner."

"I sort of remember that there was not much evidence. Her description was too weak. Unfortunately, there was the issue of her not being sober."

"Yes, she had admitted having drunk alcohol that evening. She was the only hope I had. Couldn't she somehow have forgotten this drink?"

"You have no idea with whom you were dealing. We are talking about Frank Wells. He was leading the prosecution. I can assure you he had done his homework. In fact, he dug so long until he found the client who offered her that glass of alcohol."

"How is that possible?"

"How? Quite simple. These guys are meticulous. Everyone called as witness had to be declared before the trial, so the defense and the prosecution can do their homework. Frank Wells and his big team went to the bar and spoke to every single customer leaving the bar one night, and one admitted having offered her a drink. I can bet you any money that he would have brought this guy to testify this, as evidence, had Eileen denied this fact. You know what would have happened if Eileen had denied having had a drink? It would have been far worse. Michael, you know what they call this?"

"Perjury."

"Yep, then you would have completely lost your only witness. My hands were bound when he accused her to have been drunk—I could not do anything."

"You didn't even try."

"No Michael, that is not true. I have not forgotten that particular moment; it remained as an unpleasant memory. I was about to stand up and object."

"But you didn't, I remember."

"Michael, you did not see the judge. You were facing the other way; you were looking straight at the witness. I faced the judge, I looked directly into his eyes. You do recall his name?"

"Yes, Carter."

"Exactly, the Honorable Judge Carter, indeed. The moment Eileen had admitted to having had alcohol that evening, he showed a great deal of antipathy towards her. As I wanted to stand up, he looked at me and shook his head. He had this determination in his eyes—you cannot imagine. It was an awful long time ago, but I will never forget. You just need to understand, he would have overruled it."

Michael sat there, peeking out of the large window onto the city. "I had expected better from you. You really managed to talk your way out of this today."

"I did no such thing. I did what I could, to the best of my abilities, to defend you."

"You took an oath; I hope you know what you did."

Michael stood up. He hoped not to have crossed the line with his last comment. But he wanted it to hang there, and he knew he had hit home with his parting shot. Vincent just looked at him, obviously hurt. The conversation was over. He remembered Jack's advice. *After the evidence, then we will see what the next step is.* He wondered though, at that particular moment, what it could be.

Michael left and was a bit wiser as to why he had never heard from Vincent again. He told Jack everything and his partner listened attentively as he maneuvered through the streets.

"This is indeed interesting. He was taken off the case immediately after he wanted to file for an appeal. We got some more investigation to do."

"And I never received any letter from him either, as I just said."

Jack did not respond, as if he had not listened. Michael looked at Jack, awaiting a comment. But he let it pass. A long quietness reigned in the air while he replayed the conversation he had with Vincent. Even though his lawyer had not been on the case anymore shortly after the trial, he still felt let down by him. But why, after the appeal, he was assigned elsewhere, seemed indeed very suspicious. He shook his head and wondered what more he was going to discover. He had a purpose now: to continue his quest for the truth.

CHAPTER 12

The Park

As Jack continued driving without uttering a word, Michael glanced continuously across at how Jake maneuvered the streets with one hand.

"Anything up, Michael?"

"Let's find a parking lot and you ride shotgun."

Jack peeked into his rear-view mirror and slammed the brakes, grinned, and got out. "Finally, some fun," Jack yelled as he left his side of the car, getting out. "You may as well move across now."

It was a great feeling behind the wheel. He had not forgotten how to drive, the traffic was light, and he felt secure, despite the cloudy sky. His vision was perfect. He had not strained his eyes over the years. What fascinated him most was the silence that reigned, even when he pressed the accelerator. He remembered the times when he was young, and the kick was to press the gas pedal hard to achieve a revving sound of the engine. It just did not happen here; instead, the car shot off like a rocket.

"Easy boy! Let's not get a speeding ticket. There are now radars at every corner. You cannot imagine how quickly you get caught these days." Michael released the gas pedal slightly. "I still remember the times when I did the same. We went at any speed we wanted to. Little control, no issue. It has become a lucrative business setting up all these cameras over recent years. The radars used to cost a lot, but now technology has become so cheap that they set these things up at almost every corner."

"Yeah, I see one ahead here, it is at the top of the lane. That thing hanging there, across the street."

"Right, Michael, this here is a special one. Slow down. It now scans the number plate of this car. In about five minutes we will pass another camera, same type, and then another one. What the cameras do is to send the scan of the license plate to a central system. It then measures your average speed over the distance. If you are over, then you get a letter home asking you for a fee for taking your photo of your car."

"Amazing. It recognizes the plates of your car?"

"Technology has evolved, Michael. You know, there are these smart asses who know where cameras are positioned, so they slow down when they approach them. After passing, they put the foot down again. This does not work anymore with this system when measuring your average speed."

"Incredible, what they have come up with over these years. Hey, how about his one. You are allowed to drive 100. Go 120 on the first stretch and then go 80 on the second."

Jack looked across at Michael and chuckled. "I suppose that may work, never thought about it. But you know what a drone is?"

"Yes, it existed already when I was a bit younger."

"That's right, but not like these we have today. Nowadays almost every kid has one. Instead of parents buying remote controlled cars, they now buy a drone. But the point I am trying to make here is that even drones are now used by the police for traffic surveillance. They can detect dangerous driving and speeding. They are even equipped with night vision cameras."

Michael continued to be amazed on the evolution of technology of the last few years, while he was away. It was, for him, like time travelling. However, he was not sure how to digest it all. Being free meant a new strain in life; a responsibility and having to cope with new daily routines. Apart from trying to make out what to do with the rest of his existence he would also need to face the advances in technologies. He was quite brilliant as a student and knew how to manage his personal computer. But after the last days of what Jack had been telling him, he was definitely out of date, old school.

"Over there at the crossing, turn left. Watch the oncoming traffic—you need to give way. There is no separate red light to make them stop, they call it traffic flow, trying to improve the run of the vehicle."

Michael approached the junction, slowed down, peeked into his rear-view mirror, and activated his indicator to turn left. "Thank you for this opportunity, Jack, it makes me feel human again."

He let the oncoming traffic pass and swiftly turned left. He enjoyed every moment. They got home and parked in the garage. Then Jack explained him how to charge the car.

"You load it overnight and in the morning the battery is full. No more petrol station. You know what the other advantage is?"

"What's that?"

"I don't buy anymore six-packs of beer." Jack grinned and entered the house.

The afternoon passed and the evening they spent roaming the city on foot. Michael stopped at several shop windows and shook his head in disbelief every time he saw the price tags.

"How can you afford this? What happened over the last years?"

Jack chuckled and explained the inflation-effect, as he kicked off with his usual discourse. "Many strikes and demands for wage increases had been made over the recent years, which in turn caused again prices to rise further. You can guess as people had more money the shop owners once more bumped up prices. This cycle really never ends. I find people should find contentment with what they have, rather than constantly striving for more, it is a never-ending spiral."

Michael nodded. He understood every word of the concept; he had studied the curves of demand and supply.

Another day had passed, and Michael felt more relief, starting to enjoy life. After shopping, Jack showed Michael his kitchen skills. He wanted to cook fresh to give his guest a treat. He realized that cooking was fun, if done together. In the past he always used tin food or poured some water on instant noodles.

"When you start to make something fresh, you also become more innovative, Michael. I add the fresh herbs here or the other seasoning there. And the biggest satisfaction of all, you get by sitting down, and knowing firstly that you have created something yourself, something special and unique." Jack grinned broadly by taking a few basil leaves from a plant, situated on the windowsill, and giving them to Michael to wash. "But mostly, you know you care about yourself and the person you serve. I've read a lot about diet and health. The added amount of nutrients and vitamins in fresh foods are a life booster and also make you less subject to any colds or illnesses, as it strengthens your immune system."

Michael was all excited and watched, impressed by the ability of Jack with his blue apron, across which was written in white cursive letters *cook'n live*. When all was prepared, they filled their plates and sat down to taste the creation of the chef.

"*Bon appétit*," Jack beamed, looking expectantly at Michael.

While enjoying a roasted chicken covered in oregano and herbs de Provence, together with cayenne pepper covered potatoes that had been added to the oven, they chatted away, and Jack continued giving Michael an update of the changed world. Michael relished every bite of the juicy meat and continued to lick his fingers with joy. He allowed himself a bottle of beer, alcohol-free, of course. It was ice-cold and tasted wonderful.

"I found out there is this little park, on the other side of town. I fancy taking you there, after we have eaten. You should have a stroll around."

"Anything you want, Jack, got no other plans."

As they chewed away, Jack slowed down thinking of how to formulate his next words. "It is a nice park. A lot of people sit there and enjoy the fresh air, even when the weather is cold." Jack took another chicken leg with his hands and took a big bite. With his mouth still half full, he hesitated but then blurted out, "You may see Judge Carter."

A moment of silence remained in the air. Michael stopped chewing and glanced across the table. "Why the hell would I want to see him?"

Jack realized the uneasiness but decided to press on. "You know, we need to do our homework. We agreed to this, it won't harm if you had a chat with him. You'd be surprised once more; you may find out something useful."

Michael swallowed the remains that he had in his mouth, put down his piece of chicken and grabbed his bottle without wiping his hands. He took a slow mouthful and gulped down hard, eyeing Jack with the corner of his eye. "I have the feeling you know more than you say."

Without looking up, Jack took his fork and poked at a potato. He dipped it in some sour cream, and put it slowly into his mouth, as Michael observed him closely, squinting.

Finally, Jack responded, still chewing slowly. "I think like a police officer, investigating. Really, nothing else. Talk to everyone involved, gather evidence, and then make your own conclusions. We learned a lot from Eileen and this Vincent guy. If we get nothing by talking to him, so what, but if we do, there may be another clue there, a piece of the puzzle. You will not do anything wrong, and you have nothing to fear. You are a free man now; he cannot harm you." Jack shrugged his shoulders as if it was the most natural thing that he had just proposed.

Michael continued to have this ominous feeling that Jack was indeed hiding something. It went all too smoothly. He pointed him in every direction, and everything Jack did actually made sense, and cleared up things. But there was more to this, he felt. He had not lost his touch for reading people, and his stay in prison had probably given him further experience. Michael picked up his chicken leg again, in silence, and ate until he completely cleaned the bone. He got up and went to the kitchen to wash his hands, took a towel and dried them, peering out of the window. Perhaps Jack was really that smart; he knew his business and he should be thankful to his host. He was the only person who really cared. He still, though, was not fully convinced.

"Fancy another beer? There is another one in the fridge," Jack shouted across.

Michael spun around, marched out of the kitchen past the table, and sat down on the sofa, analyzing the red carpet. He wasn't sure what to say. "Jack, please be honest, there is a lot more to this than you are telling me. You ran down the story numerous times how you studied the case, but now it seems that you are on this mission, and I am your tool."

"I wouldn't call it *my* mission, it is *yours*. I'd say I am intrigued, and I want to help you to find the truth. I am offering my help. It is you who managed to piece everything together so far. It is to you to whom Eileen opened up her heart. Do you really believe Vincent would have spoken to me?"

Jack got up, went to the kitchen, and took another beer. He then returned, sat down next to Michael and they both admired the red carpet together.

"I am not pushing you to do all this. But if you want peace of mind, you should try to get to the bottom of this. I'd talk to Judge Carter next.

Are you sure you don't want another beer?" Jack unscrewed his bottle and took a big gulp.

Half an hour later, they were almost ready after clearing up and filling the dishwasher. Jack had convinced Michael, and he accepted, reluctantly, to go ahead with his plan. "Make sure to put on a clean shirt and comb your hair for good measure. You never know who you will meet," Jack said, grinning as usual.

"I thought we are just going to go to find Judge Carter. Anybody else there to see, as well?"

Jack had already turned round with his key in his hand, ready to go. Michael had again this grim feeling that this was a little more than just a visit to Judge Carter. He would be proven right. Not today, but eventually.

CHAPTER 13

Judge Carter

They drove into a very wealthy part of town, quiet and prosperous. Big houses with large gardens all tidy and clean decorated the landscape. You could smell the money through the air conditioning. Jack stopped somewhere prior to his destination.

"I would fancy for you to speak to him on your own. I was a guard and was somehow part of his law. I would only put him off with my presence."

Michael had already guessed that his partner would decline to see Judge Carter. He listened to how to get to the park and shut the door. The procedure was the same as with Eileen and Vincent. As he got out, Jack disappeared. He had to follow the small road, turn right, and continue straight. Somewhere on the left would be a small passage to a green field. It was a posh area with high-powered vehicles, models he had never seen in such abundance. "SUVs," Jack called them, yesterday when he asked. When he was younger, he recalled only being familiar with the term Jeep. Now there were so many versions, nice ones really, he admired them all. He turned into the small passageway, passing lovely villas with greens. A particularly large mansion had a large pool, with deck chairs spread around. He paused a moment and stared. *When was the last time I swam in a pool?* he thought and then continued walking, entering the big field by a gate.

He stood there and looked around. *He will be there, sitting on a bench, reading the paper,* Jack told him. He wondered how Jack knew this particularity. He hadn't bothered asking.

As he checked his surroundings, he walked past children playing on swings and climbing frames. A big one was just to his left. Children disappeared into a big blue tube, which wound in all types of directions. Suddenly, they reappeared at the bottom, giggling, and shouting away. *I wish I had something like this when I was that age,* he smiled. As he continued on his way, he saw an old man he recognized. He had the same protruding nose, his glasses were thick-rimmed and his hair the same, combed back, just grey. He verified again left and right, to ascertain himself but saw no other elderly person.

He approached the bench, eyeing him carefully. *The Honorable Judge Carter, here we meet again.* He sat there dressed in a thick brown coat, brown trousers, and matching boots. Both of his dark-gloved hands held a newspaper. He was so absorbed studying the pages that he did not notice Michael taking a seat to his right. He dug his hands in his coat pockets, took a deep breath, and waited. *How should I start this? Stay calm, just talk.* All possible conversations kept coming up in his mind. Minutes passed as the pages turned, followed by a sporadic grunt. Eventually he found the courage to open his mouth. He was, though, still not sure what to say.

"Good afternoon!" Michael voiced, hoarse, looking into the distance ahead, as he saw another child appearing suddenly at the opening of a hole.

The judge turned his head slowly towards Michael, gave him an uninterested glance above his reading glasses and nodded. "Good morning young chap," he said, and then went back to reading, calmly as he had before, turning one page and then emitting the occasional sigh and cough.

Michael waited a few more seconds before voicing, "My name is Michael Fletcher."

You could hear the rustle of the newspaper. The old man looked up and gazed at Michael, who had not moved. Michael kept on staring straight ahead, unemotional, still with his hands tucked tightly in. It was chilly outside, but he felt his hands sweat. His emotions surged, surpassing levels he hadn't felt in years. His heart pounded faster, knowing that the person currently eyeing him had played a significant role in his extended sentence. A simmering hatred now emerged, caused by the endless mental suffering he had endured.

The judge lifted his reading glasses with his right hand and looked closer. Minutes seemed to pass.

"Mr. Fletcher," he paused and then continued, "oh, how are you? How long are you out?"

"I see you remember me."

"Well, yes of course, I do."

"Even after such a long time?"

"Well, I do tend to remember definitively all the important cases, and well, yours was quite notorious."

"Notorious, was it?"

"Well, it is a rather quiet city this one. It is not often we had cases like this."

"I see."

The judge cleared his throat. "Well, nice to know you are well. Good luck."

He got up and wanted to leave, while Michael continued to calmly remain in his position.

"Your Honor, I am here to talk. I have a few questions to ask."

The judge spun around with disgust and superiority on his face. "There is nothing really to discuss, young chap. I do not know what you want."

"To talk." Michael realized the calm attitude of the judge had left him.

"And what do you want to talk about?" His gaze focused on him narrowly.

"The case."

Judge Carter jerked back his head in a defensive way. "What about the case? I do not see what there is to talk about," he snapped. "It happened a long time ago. I am retired and I have no wish to discuss it with you."

"Well, I do." Michael noted an internal fire burning, his heart racing even faster. He jerked out his hands from his coat pocket, darted forwards and grabbed the judge by his collar, almost knocking off his glasses. The judge, still with the newspaper in one hand, was shaking slightly and looked at Michael in disbelief. He was a very tall man. He towered above the same way he had also done so in the court room, Confident, calm, and authoritarian.

"I just want to talk, okay?"

Their gazes met and Michael noticed fear in the eyes of a man that had always been one who inflicted fear on the others. The table had turned, and Michael noticed this. The judge was not as sure of himself as he had been. The judge trembled and his lips twitched as Michael continued his stronghold, looking up with determination. Their glare kept hitting each other, like two laser beams meeting, battling to move in one direction or the other.

Judge Carter tried to compose himself and breathed in. "As Judge, and part of the law of this city, let me give you one piece of advice. Let go, don't cause trouble."

"I just want to talk to you."

"And I do not wish to."

"So, tell me why?"

"Why, what?"

"Why was I convicted for such a long period of time, why so easily, why dismiss the evidence and witness so easily?"

The judge looked around, still being held by the collar. He hesitated and breathed heavily, his cheeks flushing and his mouth twitching further. "Let me give you this piece of advice. If you really want the truth, then go and try and find that runner, that jogger, whatever you want to call it. There is nothing more to tell you or discuss. Now let go of me or I will hold you for aggravation."

Michael let go. He realized he had perhaps gone too far. He watched as the judge pulled down his coat, a final stare, then spun around and walked away in long strides. Before leaving the gate, he waved at two ladies to his right, standing with their hands in their coat pockets, chatting away. They were probably spending their afternoons attending their children's play. One of them returned the wave and smiled. Carter did not stop. Then he was gone.

Michael felt good. His adrenaline was circulating after so many years of dormancy. He did not regret confronting the judge; he did nothing wrong. On the contrary, he did something he was actually longing to do for such a long time, which was getting answers. *Find the runner*, he murmured to himself, *find the runner*. It was an answer that confirmed what Eileen had seen.

He was tempted to follow Judge Carter but decided otherwise. He did not want to cause problems. He was doubtful that he could be held accountable for aggravation. He did, however, not question the authority of Carter. Even though he retired, he may have the possibility to get Michael into trouble. He stood there for a while and contemplated what Carter was trying to imply. *Let me give you one piece of advice if you really want the truth.* The truth. Was the truth never revealed? He had to tell Jack and discuss it with him, his mentor and advisor. After all, it was Jack that gave him the clues and idea how to go about the case. This morning, he was still not fully convinced if this all made sense, to dig up a case which was closed years back. Now, however, he felt the tingle to get to the bottom of this.

He went back to the bench and sat down again, rerunning the conversation in his head. He did not want to leave so quickly, fearing bumping into the judge again and decided to wait a few more minutes. He was agitated, his hands shook, and he felt his heart beating fast. Michael took a couple of deep breaths to compose himself and got up. He turned his head left and right to see if someone was watching him. After all, he had grabbed an old man by the collar. Nobody was watching him; that was good. He took a first step and walked slowly to the exit gate, ignoring the two chatting ladies to the right and shutting out the different cries of joy of the children around him. He continued past the houses he had admired so much, without peeking, his mind whirling, trying to arrange all the information which had been collected over the last days. The crime scene, his lovely afternoon with Eileen and the more disturbing meeting with Vincent. And there was another event with the judge, more rough but quite significant. More data, more clues.

Michael rounded the corner and walked to the car where Jack was sitting in his seat with his eyes closed, once again. He was about to knock on the window but remained standing still by the passenger door. *Would the judge have said something similar if there hadn't been a possibility that there was really another person?* Michael continued to stand there contemplating the significance of the encounter and then went to the driver's side and knocked on the window.

It was a long drive home; it was rush hour with a lot of stop and go. Jack guessed it was better he would drive as he listened to the account of Michael. Michael repeated the story a few times. Jack never responded, just nodded. Finally, when stopping at a set of lights he turned his head.

"Looks like you elicited little sympathy then," Jack raised one eyebrow, "I told you there is something foul. The Honorable Judge Carter knows more than he is admitting. It won't be the last time we will have seen him; I tell you. You will need to certainly pay him another visit. Now we have only warmed up."

What bee has he got in his bonnet? Michael thought and looked across surprisingly at Jack. It bothered him that there was something Jack was hiding. Finally, after a while, he asked. "What can I achieve by seeing him again? He does not want to talk to me."

"Not initially, but you'd be surprised what you can achieve with some persistence. Ever seen this German TV crime series called *Derrick* with Horst Tappert?"

"What has that to do with this?"

"Have you seen it, Michael?"

"Of course, I have, it is famous all over the world."

"There you are. You know why the detective always solved the mysteries, even though the obvious murderer never wanted to speak to him?"

"Enlighten me."

"Because he kept on meeting him, over and over again. His most famous sentence was always, 'Oh I just want to get to know you.' He kept on engaging, talking, and seeing the killer until he eventually opened up. That is exactly what you have to do. Make him talk by standing on his feet. You'd be surprised what you can achieve."

Michael looked across once more with his eyes wide open and bewildered. He pondered on what Jack said, looking again blankly at the road ahead. He asked himself the question he had already asked so many times: *Why hadn't all this been investigated initially before the process?* He was not convinced. How can he, a detainee and an ex-guard carry out an investigation that had been filed away years back? He had heard of all the advances in cases of the past that had been solved many years later, using new indications and advanced technologies, such as DNA evidence. But in this case, it was an investigation into finding another suspect. The knife was clean. There were no other traces on the weapon apart from his prints.

Michael shook his head. "I doubt that even *Derrick* would be able to solve this case."

"Well, Michael, then we have to be cleverer than *Derrick*. What was his assistant's name?"

"Harry Klein."

"Yes, that's him. So, you are?"

"Very funny." Michael felt himself almost smile.

"As I am the driver and you are the person who sits next to me …" Jack chuckled and then guffawed at his own remark, so he did not bother to finish the sentence, wiping a tear of laughter from his right eye.

From where does he get all his humor? Michael thought to himself. He was, though, glad that Jack was so whimsy. It did him good and helped to cheer him up. He needed to loosen up and become more positive. Jack had the right attitude and he understood he simply needed to adapt.

They rounded up the day with a light dinner and another evening walk before Michael rested and fell asleep, uneasy, as his encounter with the judge had troubled him.

CHAPTER 14

Brian

In the morning they went for a walk and were having a small snack for lunch to discuss the plans for the day. Jack made avocado again, which Michael liked so much, mixed with cherry-tomatoes and a squeeze of lemon, salt & pepper, together with warm bread from the bakery.

"So, let's resume what we have so far," Jack said with a full mouth, chewing away excitedly. "First of all, we have Eileen, who confirms that there was someone unusual running past her. Judge Carter does not seem to deny this. In fact, he gave the hint again. Whether he just said it to get rid of you we do not know. But there must be something that kept this in the back of his mind. Secondly, your prison sentence was too long, well, sorry to mention this." Jack looked up, but Michael did not respond. "This Vincent, your old lawyer, suddenly disappeared. Let's say he was asked to disappear, that is a better formulation. In any case, nobody replaced him. I find that highly odd. Thirdly, the fact that the judge was so hard on you during the trial and did nothing really to support the theory of Eileen or of the possible involvement of another person that fled from the scene. So basically, we have the missing person, the disappearance of Vincent and the strange behavior of the judge."

"Nothing to add, I would say, Harry."

"Harry? Ha, good one. You are definitely becoming more relaxed." Jack chewed away amusingly. "Good, now we have made a summary. What is the next step. What would you do, Derrick?"

Michael also chuckled and thought. "I would like to see Eileen again. I also want to ask her if she thinks it may have been a man or a woman. Asking for further description again will not help, but I will try. Also, I like her muffins and she is a lovely person. I like *her* a lot. She reminds me of my mother, of a time ago. She is very eager for me to meet her husband; they seem to be very happily married. I adore that family. They have a positive influence on me, do you understand? They cheer me up."

"Of course, it makes sense. It is amazing how people's happiness can make you content. If someone is miserable, you also become miserable. Happiness can be transmitted, the same as sadness. I know all about it," Jack said with a somber tone. "When I am with my daughter, she laughs all the time, so guess what I do, I laugh with her. It is contagious. Have you ever heard of laughing yoga?"

"What is that?"

"You know what yoga is?"

"Yes, relaxing your body, meditation, breathing, a bit of everything that makes you feel good."

"Yes, yoga makes you feel good, it helps you. Of course, laughter and happiness also make you feel good. So, what they do during laughing yoga is laugh all the time, deliberately. You cannot call it forced but intentionally, through different relaxing exercises. They found that this type of laugher is just as healthy as spontaneous laughter."

"Interesting."

"You know why kids always laugh?"

"I can imagine, but tell me, now that you are giving the story line," Michael responded, smiling.

Jack grinned. "Kids laugh more than we do because they have no worries. They simply do not question if something is funny. They just want to have fun while adults are simply too busy and concerned with daily life to have time to have fun. Most of all, we are afraid of appearance and question everything we do. We lack spontaneousness. I would say, we are afraid to be criticized."

Michael thought and nodded. "You are right. I have worried for the last twenty-six years; I have had no reason to be happy and laugh. No wonder I felt miserable all time."

"There you are. That is why I am trying to cheer you up. And going to see Eileen, as you said, also makes you happy. You are happy if you are with joyful people." Michael nodded approvingly. "Well, that is then settled, you will see Eileen again. What would be the next step, after seeing her?"

"Next, well, we spoke about Tom Bane, remember him? I do not think he knows much, but I am curious why I never heard from him again."

"Great, now we have two next steps. Let us gobble up and I will make us a chamomile tea, it is also good to reduce stress and alleviate anxiety. Then I suggest we go and try to see Eileen, perhaps she is in."

After lunch they headed out and Michael was again allowed to drive. They stopped somewhere close to Eileen's and then Jack retook the wheel, watching as Michael walked to house number 194 on Winston Road.

Michael wasn't sure if she was in, so he decided to give the house bell two lengthy and well-spaced pushes. He did not have to wait too long, as Eileen was already at the door after he released the button the second time. She opened it and received him with a big smile.

"Oh, hello Mr. Fletcher! No, it is *Michael* now!" Another tight and lengthier hug followed. This time he had the courage to also embrace her. He felt her warmth and closed his eyes for a moment, feeling like a little boy being cuddled by his mother. She smiled at him.

"Please, do come in, I am so glad to see you once again. You just missed my husband. He was called a few minutes ago by a customer. He shouldn't be long. I told him that you had passed by. He was actually quite eager to meet you. Let me fix you a cup of coffee, with milk and sugar, I remember. I have also baked those muffins again; you enjoyed them so much last time. So nice of you to come and see me. Being retired is not all that great. I do miss the contacts. You cannot imagine how much chit-chat there was when I was working at the bar. Highly interesting!"

He entered again the nicely furnished home feeling welcomed, and admired once more a fresh set of Lilies, emitting the same fragrance as the last time. He smiled, closed his eyes, and took a deep breath. Eileen was working in the kitchen as he walked around the living room, looking at different family pictures. He recognized Eileen's son. Justin, he recalled. Also, her husband was in the photo holding a fishing rod in one hand and a fish on the hook in the other. He did not know his name. He did not recall Eileen mentioning it. "Do they go fishing often?" he called across the room.

Eileen came in with a tray and smiled broadly. "Oh, occasionally. You are looking at a quite recent photo. Whenever Justin comes to see us, Brian decides to take him on a fishing trip. There is a river not far from here. It is a new hobby of Brian's. He is so awfully proud and of course wants to share his skill with Justin. I myself am not so fond of this sport, if you want to call it that. All day sitting there and waiting for something to bite. Much easier to just go and buy something. Mind you, fish has become tremendously expensive, so I suppose fishing for free is not such a bad idea."

Well, at least now he also knew the name of Eileen's husband. He continued to admire the family pictures and then went to the table where he saw everything perfectly set out for an afternoon coffee and cake.

She wore a bright sweater and faded jeans. Her hair was once more tied into a bun, this time on top of her head. A long red wooden hairpin had been stuck through the bunch to hold them together and it made her look more beautiful than ever.

"I like your hair; it is very elegant."

"Thank you, Michael. Last night we went for sushi. I stole this one here," Eileen said, smiling, pointing at the pin in her bun. Michael was not sure what to say. "Hey, cheer up, just kidding. I wanted to be funny." Eileen smiled brightly as she pulled a chair from the dining room table and offered it to Michael.

"Let's have some fun while you're here," she said, smiling as she came from the kitchen again with the last plates. She went to the sideboard and from the middle drawer took out a pack of cards. "I assume you know blackjack. I am rather good at it; I play quite often with friends."

He smiled. *I am better.* But with a pack where you reshuffle every time, the advantage is gone. Counting cards was not possible. They played away and Eileen won most of the time. Occasionally they stopped and ate, gossiped, and laughed. Michael had two refills of coffee.

"Ten and ace," Eileen laughed. Michael enjoyed himself and was happy to be here. Every time he looked up, memories of the past reappeared, his mother facing and smiling at him. Eileen had not just the same look but was just as kind and compassionate. The nice memory popped quickly though; it was a memory of the far past. He wondered whether it was the influence of his father that his mother cut all the leads. He was brought back to reality when he heard a door unlock and a man walked in. He wore a baseball cap and a thick jacket and scarf. He grinned broadly with wide eyes at Michael and shook his hands.

"Finally, I guess you must be Mr. Fletcher. Oh no, card games, has Eileen been bothering you with these?"

"Not at all. I had a lot of fun actually, Mr. Parker. I enjoyed myself playing."

"Jolly good, I am glad, and do please call me Brian."

"I am Michael, real joy to meet you."

"A cup of coffee for you, darling?" Eileen immediately jumped up.

"Yes please, sweetheart," Brian answered, grinning even more, taking off his scarf and jacket.

Michael liked being here increasingly. They were such a warm, kind, and loving family. He was thrilled, and his heart felt at peace.

"Michael let's take a seat on the sofa and chat. I am curious. I am really sorry about what happened to you. If there is anything we can do, we would like to help." Brian sat down and tapped with his hand the place next to him. Eileen disappeared into the kitchen, to fetch the cup of coffee.

"So, tell me Michael, how are you coping right now? Where are you staying?"

"I am at a friend's place currently; he is putting me up."

"Well, that is nice of him. Eileen has been talking about you nonstop since you came here a few days ago. We are both so sorry … thank you, sweetheart," Brian voiced as he was handed his cup of coffee. "Eileen is one-hundred percent certain that there was someone else running from the scene. She kept speaking about nobody else for weeks, even months, after the trial. Still today she talks about it when she comes back from town after seeing some of her friends at that bar."

Michael listened and then the important question popped up in his mind. "May I ask you a question, Eileen?"

"Please go ahead." Eileen sat down opposite them on a chair, looking at Michael expectantly.

"The person you saw–was it definitely a man, or could it have been a woman?"

"I am certain about that. A man. Surely. The way he ran and panted, very ugly, no woman could do that."

Michael thought about it. *Well then, that question is now answered.* "And the size, I remember you said, was not much different to me."

"Yes, about your size, maybe a bit smaller, but more or less like you, as far as I can remember. That image keeps coming up repeatedly. Then I continued walking and I saw you, trying to help that poor boy."

"Eileen went to his funeral. Didn't you tell our guest, sweetheart?"

"No, I haven't yet. Poor Flynn Meier, I went to the funeral. Quite a number of people attended, but I did not recognize many. I was somewhere at the back and the congregation was so big that I did not even see really see what went on at the front."

Michael nodded. "Where is this place where was he buried?" He did not know why he asked this question, but he thought it might not harm, to know.

"There is only one place in town, north end, about 20 minutes by car."

"So really not far then." Michael paused for a while and pondered about all the people who had attended; they had all blamed him. He felt a sense of uneasiness again and gripped his left hand with his right as he suddenly felt a slight tremble. Brian sensed that something was wrong and placed a caring hand on his right hand.

After a glass of water, he felt better, and they continued chatting along. He told them about certain good memories of the prison time when he helped inmates such as Fernando finish school but tried to leave out the more unpleasant episodes of loneliness and solitude.

"Well, I am so glad you are settling well into your new life now. I propose not next but the week after, you come here, as Justin will visit us for the weekend. I have planned a fishing day. You must come along. What do you say?"

"That is kind of you. I gladly accept."

"What we do is clean the fish and Eileen pops it into the oven, enrobed with basic herbs in tin foil. It is delicious, I can assure you. She also adds potatoes. She is a great cook. You will love her soy sauce-fried bell peppers, blended with Chinese chili sauce."

"I am already looking forward to it." Michael felt a tinge of happiness. It is what he needed; exactly what Jack had explained to him the very morning.

By the time he knew it, the afternoon had gone and it was getting dark. He felt so welcome he had totally forgotten that Jack was still waiting in the car somewhere outside. "I so much enjoyed coming here. I feel so welcome, thanks so much for your kindness, but I need to head off, it is getting late. The friend I am staying with is waiting for me."

"Well, you are welcome indeed. Do you need a ride? I have to drive off with my Taxi again anyway."

"No thank you, that is kind. I will walk."

"Okay then, well do come again, and remember, Saturday, not the next but the week after. Come at eight in the morning, or earlier if you wish. The earlier the better the fish tend to bite." Michael smiled and nodded. "It was really nice to speak to you. And if you wish, of course you are welcome any other time, just drop in. Eileen can make something special for you to eat."

"Too kind of you. Thank you. I will surely pass by to see you often."

Michael got a warm handshake and even a small hug from Brian, and a big one plus a kiss on the cheek from Eileen. He almost burst into tears. Emotions were taking over; he had not felt so much warmth and kindness for a long time. He tried to suppress them though, as he felt a touch of embarrassment.

Michael walked away slowly and then picked up speed. He had actually forgotten Jack completely, as he had been so absorbed in the discussions. As he rounded the corner, Jack was not there. He stood there for a while and reflected on what to do. He knew more or less where he lived. Perhaps he should go back and ask Brian for a ride after all. He kept waiting and then turned round and started walking again to the house of Eileen as a car with flashing lights approached. It was Jack.

"Hi Michael, jump in. Sorry not to have been waiting for you. I just quickly did some shopping. I guessed you would be a while, so I thought to take the opportunity. How did it go?"

Michael reported everything that was discussed, as well as the fact that Eileen was certain to exclude that it was a woman. Jack listened without interrupting.

"Do you know where Flynn Meier is buried?"

Jack did not respond. There was a longer silence. Michael wanted to repeat the question, but Jack, acting as if he needed to think, finally said, "No idea."

"At the cemetery, here in town, you know where it is?"

"Yes, that place I know, there is only one, it is not far."

"That is where we should go next, tomorrow."

"You want to go and see where he is buried? Why is that?"

"No idea. I think I owe it to him. I was the last to possibly see him alive."

"If you say so."

Jack kept quiet for a while driving home. Then he burst out suddenly, again full of energy. "For dinner tonight, as I said, I did some shopping."

"Sounds great, what are you making?"

"Me? No, us. You need to learn to cook as well," Jack winked at Michael, who returned a smile, quite excited.

Dinner was great and Michael repeated the whole story again of his evening with Eileen and Brian. As they ate seabass simmered in white wine, olive oil-fried mushrooms and long peppers, Michael was reminded of the photos that Eileen had displayed in her living room. He told Jack about Brian's fishing passion and the invitation he got to join him. Jack somehow agreed with Eileen–it was indeed a bit easier to buy the fish. As long as you knew where to go, you could get some really fresh stuff. They chatted away and Michael excused himself to get a good night's rest, as the previous night was not so peaceful for him. They decided, though, to first take a short walk outside to help the digestion and finally, after some fresh air and further exchanges of the day's events, Michael went to sleep, fully relaxed and joyful. It was a nice ending to the day for him.

CHAPTER 15

The Cemetery

The following day, after a light breakfast, they got ready and drove off to the cemetery. Michael sat again behind the wheel, Jack watching to be certain that he obeyed all traffic regulations. He maneuvered confidently through the streets, following directions. It was a nice feeling behind the wheel again. He enjoyed himself and brought back a sense of self-esteem. He needed to regain it; he knew, however, that it would take time. *One step at a time,* he said to himself. *Give me time and I will rebuild the world.* He wondered where he got this one from.

Finally, they arrived at an empty parking lot and walked to the entrance. "It will take us hours to find his grave. Is there no way on these modern phones to look it up?"

Jack chuckled. "Data privacy protection, at least around here."

Michael wondered what that meant as he pushed the heavy wrought iron gate and stepped into the cemetery. "I suppose we got all day. It isn't raining and we have nothing else to do."

"Yep." Jack followed slowly, closing the gate behind him.

The sandy and partially grassy ground was moist but solid. The sounds of their footsteps were entirely muffled, and a complete stillness reigned as they ambled along. They marched past various graves, most of them arranged in blocks of four, to be able to gain access to each individual tomb from the sides. Some of them were freshly piled up, while some were older and the occasional was beautifully decorated with recently laid flowers. The mortuary had shrunk over the years and was not all so big as in the past. Many people preferred cremations these days and then also decided not to bury their ashes. Instead, the loved ones were taken in urns to the sea or to wherever their favorite spot had been. There the ashes could be spread or laid down.

They kept on walking and sometimes had the impression that they were going around in circles. Michael was certain to have seen several names more than once. However, he could not orient himself only on names, as these were indeed repetitive. Family names were quite common. Even Fletcher he had seen more than once. He was certain that they were unlikely to be related. His family came from another part of the country.

More than two hours had passed already. Occasionally they stopped and admired centerpieces, sculptures, or other monuments spread across the cemetery. Finally, Michael stopped and pointed.

"There it is, Flynn Meier." He strode towards the grave and stopped in front of it. Solemnly, he regarded the tomb and interlocked his fingers in prayer in front of him. Jack slowly caught up and stepped next to him, his arms folded. There was a large grey chiseled headstone, probably of granite, quite big and nicely shaped. Two big grey flowerpots with azalea shrubs were placed on either side. On the stone under a black iron cross was written: *In loving memories.* Underneath was *Flynn Meier,* and the dates of the deceased: *9 July 1968 – buried 28 February 1996.* Michael read and reread the dates.

"Well, I do not need to do the math. It's about twenty-six years ago the burial took place," Michael said self-sarcastically. He wondered again how much he was really accountable for this death. It was certainly a creepy feeling, and a cold shiver ran down his back. He was the last to have seen him alive. What could he have done differently at the time? This was a personal question he had asked himself more than once. Even though he had no reason to feel any guilt, he felt it now more than ever. Flynn had probably died in his arms due to his uncoordinated move of turning him on his back, aided by his state of inebriation.

They continued to remain standing for minutes without uttering a word, just staring at the grave and the name.

"What shall I say to him, Jack?"

"Well, a quiet prayer would do."

In his mind he told the Lord's Prayer. He had often joined Fernando in worship, his dear student in prison. Fernando came from a deeply religious family and prayed three times a day. He explained that praying often opened your soul, it allowed you to say things either to yourself or to God that normally you could not utter to another person. You were able to liberate yourself from the worries and anxieties and unblock something hidden that you were not even aware of, something stuck deep inside. This way it allowed you to also forgive yourself and others, loosening a personal burden. Fernando explained that forgiveness was an important part of their family belief. Michael therefore understood why Fernando's family welcomed him back home, fully absolved. Then he remembered again his own parents and wondered if they would ever forgive.

Moments passed as Michael finished his prayers. "Amen. What now?"

Jack did not answer. He seemed fully absorbed as well. But finally, he said in a low voice, "Well, at least we found him. So, good question, we know now where he is buried."

"Yes, but it doesn't help." He stood there and read the name on the gravestone again. On the left, on the same stone, were two other names, which meant little to Michael. "Marta and George Hayden, I wonder who they are," he said in a solemn voice. "Not the same name, odd. Probably some relative."

"Could be," Jack responded slowly.

"Certainly not direct relatives, they have a different name. The boys tend to carry down the name of the generations."

"Marta and George could have had a daughter or granddaughter, and she married Meier. What do you say?"

His brow furrowed in thoughts. "Possibly. So, he could be some son in law perhaps. Mrs. Meier is definitely not here." Michael contemplated a bit more on the significance of what he had just said, then looked across at Jack. "Don't even try to mention it!"

"What?" Jack said in a serious tone.

"I know you. Do not propose to find Mrs. Meier, no way. I am not going to face her. She will probably eat me alive. And I cannot apologize to her for something I did not do. What could I possibly say to her?"

"I agree with you here, Michael. Would be a bit tasteless. What could you say to her? 'Sorry, Mrs. Meier, about what happened, but I didn't do it.' Well, that could be a start, but on the other hand you are right. She would not be happy to see you and ask you to leave, without any further ado, or might jump and strangle you."

Michael looked again at Jack and shook his head. "Well, let us not go that far. It was a long time ago."

"Inner grief may never disappear."

Michael did not like the discussion, so decided to simply keep quiet. They continued to stand there for a while. He made his cross with his right hand—first forehead, chest, then left and then right. He then spun around, eyeing Jack again, who was still standing there motionless with his arms folded.

"Coming or staying?"

"Be along. Give me a second, please. I am a bit sentimental at times."

Michael nodded and started striding away, slowly, occasionally looking over his shoulder eyeing Jack. He didn't like these types of places much. An overwhelming wave of sadness and suffering enveloped him. Releasing a loved one was undoubtedly a daunting task; he, too, had experienced the painful act of being cast aside by his parents. The memory of this realization inflicted a sudden pang, intensifying the inner turmoil. He took a deep breath in an attempt to compose himself, but he couldn't prevent tears from streaming down his cheeks. What he held back often for twenty-six years came out. He did dearly miss them, and he couldn't comprehend how they could have completely disowned him in such a drastic manner. He found a tissue, wiped his cheeks, blew his nose, and breathed in deeply. Two big baskets for greens and old flowers were lined up on the way to the exit. He tossed his tissue into the first and exited the grounds past the iron gate.

Michael waited outside for another ten minutes, then Jack finally appeared. They got into the car without any comments and rode off. The only thing making a sound was the radio playing, and they started to relax again.

They listened to various songs, just enjoying the music, forgetting for the moment their worries.

"Who is she?" Michael asked curiously at one moment.

"Sounds like *Lady Gaga*."

"Never heard of her. Great beat."

"Yeah, one of the biggest pop stars on earth. Extremely talented, extremely successful. Became famous more than ten years ago."

Michael once more realized he had been living in another world, away from reality. He watched the fields and the scattered elm trees decorating the horizon. The scenery was beautiful, the sun shone, and birds were flying around, busy gathering grass, moss, and thin twigs, to start building nests for their offspring. A new breeding place and a home was being prepared for a new generation. All he had now was the home of Jack. No other place to go. For how long he would be able to stay had never been a discussion point; eventually, it would probably come up.

"Let me go and see Tom Bane tomorrow, what do you say?" Michael suddenly blurted out.

"Good idea, but I will definitely stay clear. I was a guard, a jailor; I really do not want to face him again."

"Well, you did nothing wrong. You just did nights."

"True, but as I said last time, you never know what they say behind your back. By the way, I know where Tom works."

"How do you know that so quickly?"

"I already checked up on him many years back. He has a quite well-known and huge car dealership called *Banes* or something similar. I guessed it from the surname, that it must be him. I went on their website to check it out. My assumption was right. You can see him next to someone else, posing among numerous cars. I recognized his face."

"Just tell me how I get there, and I will find it myself."

"I propose I take you and I disappear. Then you figure out yourself how to get back to my place. How is that as a challenge?"

"Deal. More or less, I know where you live now, after all the walking we have done."

"So that is agreed then. Now let us go to the fish market since it is still open. You liked the seabass yesterday?"

"It was delicious."

"Good. Let us see what they have. Yesterday I also saw some great salmon. Fry it in olive oil with onions and garlic, then deglaze it with white wine."

"What does 'deglaze' mean?"

"Simply add a bit of white wine at the end, not too much. It gives a nice gravy. Let it simmer and it thickens a bit, together with the onions and garlic. You can also add a couple of cherry tomatoes."

"Wonderful. We should open a small restaurant."

"What was that play of words again about the Duke and the Grand Duke?"

Michael chucked. "I didn't catch it."

They arrived at a parking lot in front of a marketplace called Fresh Food. Michael wanted to get out but was held back by Jack checking his phone and doing some manipulations.

"Wait a minute. I suggest you give Tom a call and do not appear without an appointment."

"Why is that?"

"Well, we do not know if he is in, has clients or is out there driving the latest model when you suddenly appear. Here is the number. Just found it on the Internet. Just press *dial*, here." Jack pointed at the place with his finger and handed it over.

Michael took it, pressed the button, and let it ring. "Banes Automobile here, how may I help?" a pleasant voice answered almost at once.

"Hmm, my name is Michael Fletcher, and I would like to speak to Mr. Tom Bane, please."

"One moment please, Mr. Fletcher," an attractive female voice echoed through the speaker.

A minute passed, then he heard a click. "Hey Michael! Is that really you? Michael, the chess guy?"

"Hi Tom, nice to hear your voice. Yes, it is me, the chess guy."

"Boy, so surprised to hear from you, where are you?"

"In town, and just calling to see if I can drop by these days."

A few seconds passed without a sound. Finally, Tom answered, "Yes sure, when?"

"How about tomorrow?"

A longer moment passed. Michael glanced at the phone and looked across at Jack, wondering if the connection had gone. Jack smiled and lifted his index finger, placing it on his lips, indicating to be simply patient. Sometimes silence was the best way to get someone to speak. Jack had learned the technique as police officer. They called it *the awkward silence.* A psychologist explained once to him on a seminar that such silences are associated with feelings of anxiety. It is not in the nature of the human to face each other and not to say anything. Eventually the weaker succumbs to feelings of uneasiness and the need to speak. This method didn't always work but was quite often successful in interrogations.

Eventually they heard a noise. "In the morning will do for you? Let us say eleven o'clock. My brother is out with a client, so we can talk. I have an appointment only at one."

"Great, I will be there."

"Do you know how to find me?"

"Sure, I will find the Banes Automobile somehow."

"Okay, see you then." He heard a click before he could say anything further to Tom.

"See you tomorrow then Tom," Michael said, while handing the phone back to Jack who made sure the call was ended. He grinned and slipped his phone into the inside pocket of his jacket, smiling even more widely than before. "Well, that went well, indeed."

"He did not sound very convinced."

"I am not surprised; did you hear his pregnant silence and how quickly he hung up? Something is up, simply not right here Michael, I tell you. You, appearing like a ghost of the past. He was not pleased at all." Jack lifted the door latch, grinning broadly again, and got out.

Michael watched him and remained seated. Before closing the door, Jack bent down to see if his partner got out. "Want to have a nap or get something to eat?"

"Coming, Jack, coming." Michael also got out, following swiftly, as Jack had already started to disappear at the entrance of a big hall.

They roamed the market for a catch of the day and watched how a fishmonger was professionally filleting salmon. He explained that it was caught while migrating back up the river to its birthplace to spawn.

"You won't get anything fresher. I caught this one here personally this morning. Most tend to go back to their birthplace, spawn, make offspring, and then die of exhaustion. Some make it back to their normal habitat. It depends on the distance they travel. Quite remarkable how well they orient themselves across the country, getting back to their original birthplace." They both nodded at the explanation and took a freshly sliced fillet. "Good for your Vitamin D, sirs, when there is little sun. Helps your skin."

Michael hoped that the seller was not referring to him. He indeed lacked the sunlight after so many years inside; his skin was rather pale. They continued, and on the way out, past a vegetable stand, they took a few bright red and yellow bell peppers and also some mushrooms.

They spent the early evening buzzing away in the kitchen. Michael followed all the instructions that Jack gave him, while Jack occasionally consulted his little smartphone to get the steps right.

"So easy is cooking, just follow what they say. You'd be amazed what variety there is. Nowadays you also find all sorts of celebrities doing these cooking shows. It is a new hype. Sincerely, I prefer not to follow everything they say and try a bit here and there. Develop your own style. But the basic instructions are always good to have."

"Whatever you say, chef."

They sat down and enjoyed every bite. Michael appreciated much more what he ate, as he cooked it, and it made him hungry; a personal feeling of self-satisfaction enrobed him. He had really created this meal, of course with some help, but it was his achievement, he was immensely proud and felt a tingle of happiness.

Michael was gradually acclimating to a contemporary way of life, embracing the nuances of this modern era. The world had certainly changed a lot with all the advances in technology over the last years. But he could adjust and learn. He was not afraid to take the challenge, and he had Jack, of course, to help him.

Take a small step and then another. With many small steps you get further, Jack had said to him as they took another walk before settling down again on the patio.

Jack arrived with two beers, alcohol free, opened the top, handed one to Michael, and made himself comfortable under a blanket. It was still not the right temperature to be able to sit a long time outside without the necessary protection for warmth. But they enjoyed the freshness of the evening.

"How are you feeling these days, Michael?"

"Well, Jack, let me say that I still need to get accustomed to being out of prison. It was a long time. It is not natural for me to sit here, to drink a beer, knowing that I could get up any moment and simply just walk to town, or go to the cinema, following any whim I have. Visiting people like Eileen and Brian is important for me to simply learn to socialize again. In prison it was always with a hint of uncertainty, not knowing what you should say or not. You were never free, neither personally, nor in your speech."

"I understand, that is natural, it will take some time to adjust." Jack took a sip and then continued while Michael enjoyed a small pensive moment. "How are you sleeping these days?"

"It's been getting better, but it's still a rough road. What still frightens me is that when I wake up, I am haunted by the trauma of my time locked away. I haven't fully adjusted to everyday life yet. Last night, I panicked in the dark and thought I was back in my cell."

"To adjust to any environment, it's important to give yourself time and not rush your inner system. Stay calm and allow yourself to adapt at your own pace. Remain active, as your day-to-day activities will help you to adjust. You really need to teach your body that now, it is living a different life in a free world."

"Yep, suppose so." Michael took his first sip and watched Jack. He held his bottle with one hand and was again in his usual pensive mode, fixating on something on the wooden paneled floorboard. He recognized the special expression that Jack took when attacking a delicate topic. He took another sip and just waited for the question to come. He did not need to wait for long.

"So, what is your plan tomorrow, at Tom's? What style are you going to adopt?"

Michael was not sure what he meant by *style*. "You can imagine I am more than upset with Tom. I really would like to know why I never heard another word from him. I am getting this feeling that everyone who I was in touch with disappeared. Vincent disappeared. The judge is evasive. I wonder why everyone is getting out of my way."

"Well, I am not."

"Thank you, Jack. I do not know how to thank you for everything you have done for me."

"That's OK. I enjoy your company. We get along well." Jack took his next sip and then continued. "Don't be shy when you speak to him. Be friendly, but straight-forward. If he told you he would contact you again once he was out, but then you never heard from him again, there must be a reason. Tom was not that type of person. He was a jolly fellow, I recall."

"Possibly. Let us see what he says."

They continued to enjoy the evening and the freshness of the air. Michael was grateful for the companionship. After years of being alone, he wasn't used to having someone around all the time. Now he could simply look up and ask a question. But in prison, he was often on his own, with nobody to talk to or consult. So, he would save up a queue of questions for his night visits with Jack. Unfortunately, by the time the visits came around, he had forgotten many of them and had to wait for the next day to ask.

Michael went to bed early and hoped to get a good night's rest for the new day ahead. His sleep had been improving; it was deeper, and he woke up less often. However, if he remained awake, his mind would ponder about the difficulties he had to face in life. Despite these worries, he also found himself picturing vivid images of opportunities that could arise. He envisioned himself and Jack becoming detectives, pairing up as investigators for wrongly incarcerated prisoners. At other times, he imagined himself cooking as a chef in a restaurant. As he entertained the wildest possibilities for his new life, his mind raced for a few hours more with excitement and anticipation. Finally, as he calmed down, he found peace and slipped back into unconsciousness to rest peacefully for the remainder of the night.

CHAPTER 16

Tom Bane

They had a longer breakfast and were in no rush. Jack prepared the table with all types of inviting and healthy dishes. They sipped their coffee for some time before they got themselves ready to head for the car dealership. Jack asked Michael mockingly if he could try to get a good deal for a sportscar. Next time Michael wanted to drive, he could have some more fun than with the Prius, out somewhere in the countryside, where there were no speed cameras.

Jack dropped Michael off on a busy road on the outskirts of town. "Remember not to go too easy on him. Dig deep and see what you can find."

"Certainly, boss."

"Are you sure you can get back on your own?"

"I will be fine. I more or less know the direction you live. Once I am getting close by, I will recognize the area. I have all day and good footwear. I need the exercise." He closed the door and watched as Jack drove away.

He strode down the sidewalk and saw a huge banner suspended on a large vertical pole. It read in bright red italic colors on a white background, *Banes Automobile*. In the distance he saw Jack disappearing as he turned a corner.

He entered the Bane Car Dealership and arrived at a small front shop. There he was welcomed and then escorted by a very smart-looking secretary to the first floor. He guessed it was probably her he spoke to yesterday. Now he had a face to put to the voice. He was by no means disillusioned. Her voice matched her body. Her hair was braided, and she wore a tight black skirt, dark tights, and white high heels. A black stripe ran down from her tights to the bottom of her heel, making her socks unite visually with her shoes. Michael could not take his eyes off her as she walked majestically up the stairs, him following just behind her. She blinked with both eyes at him as she knocked on *The Manager* door and let the guest enter. Michael was so overwhelmed that he did not even notice that Tom was already standing there grinning with his arms wide open. He only came back to reality, still smelling the scent of her cherry lipstick, when the door shut behind him.

They embraced and Tom kept smiling. "Great to see you, do come in and have a seat," he said pleasantly in a soft tone as he waved at an expensive leather armchair. Michael did not hesitate and made himself comfortable while Tom checked that the door was fully shut, walked around a light brown maple wood desk, and placed himself in an equally comfortable dark leather swivel chair with a high back, facing his guest.

"I see you are doing well, Tom," Michael said, looking around. The walls were covered by portraits of various luxury cars. They were models he had never seen and did not even imagine existed.

"Oh, more appearance, you know. Remember what they say: 'The client is king.' Better make him feel great before squeezing all the money out of him. What counts is that he buys the most expensive car, with all the extras, of course."

Michael eyed him carefully. Tom had aged, with many wrinkles and white streaks. "So, Tom Bane, from a lawyer to a car dealer, is it?"

"Let me be honest, it is my brother's business. After getting out, he needed someone to run the office and do the paperwork and the taxes for the company. As I was expunged, I was legally entitled to work as a lawyer again. My license, though, had run out, after such a long absenteeism. I did not want to go through all the reeducation and long procedures again. So, I opted for the easy way out. My brother needed someone trustworthy, so who else than somebody from prison," Tom blurted out with laughter. Michael avoided any smirk. "I am family after all, mind you. So, he decided to give me this job. It goes rather well, and I meet a lot of people. It is sort of fun and also interesting. And my pay is not bad at all. I am the second boss here, so whenever my brother is driving around a high-powered car with a client, I take this room, just to impress someone. You saw the secretary–gives me time to be alone with her!" Tom smiled and raised his eyebrows.

Michael did not react. He came for another reason to see his old acquaintance, someone he had trusted, but who had let him down. Now he seemed to be chatting away as if nothing had happened, or as if they had been great old buddies. He wanted the conversation to go in another direction and kept quiet. He had learned that patience is a virtue. Then Tom turned the conversation around on his own by asking, "Anyway, how about you? Please tell me everything."

"Well, I've been out for a couple of days. I now live with Jack Feller. You remember him probably, the night guard." Tom raised his eyebrows in surprise, but just kept silent and nodded. "Well, I am sort of roaming around and I am trying to come up with different clues as to what may have occurred and what led to my long incarceration. I am not really able to let go of what happened."

Tom continued to peer at his visitor, perplexed. He leaned back, listening. Michael hesitated, then finally said, "So Tom, why did you never come and visit me in prison?"

Tom bit his lower lip and took a deep breath, feeling noticeably uncomfortable. He got up, went to the window and looked out, pushing his left hand into his trouser pocket while pointing at something outside with the other. Michael looked up and wondered why Tom had turned his back to him.

It was a while, then Tom finally said, "See that huge parking lot over there?" Michael noticed a sarcastic smile as Tom quickly glanced at him.

He got up from his seat and walked up to the window and peered out, to where Tom was pointing. Tom put his other hand in his pocket and continued.

"Ten acres, about forty-thousand square meters. You know how much it cost us?" he asked in a peculiar way, still peering out.

Michael stood there for a while, trying to clear his thoughts. The tone and the way Tom posed the question startled him; he understood it was not a casual question. He squinted his eyes and contemplated what to say while scanning the large area covered by hundreds of cars. He did not want to look Tom in the eyes. He got used to paying attention and interpreting what people were saying without using a sign of facial expressions. He had done this for the last twenty-six years listening to Jack, through that square opening in the door. This way he could concentrate better.

"I guess nothing, Tom, I think I am getting the picture."

Tom's smile vanished as quickly as it appeared, and he looked seriously at Michael. "Damn right you are. You are very smart. It was on the condition that I would stay clear of you. It was the deal. I was prohibited from seeing you. My brother would not have gotten it without that condition."

A moment of uncomfortable silence remained in the room. Only the roaring of a car was heard outside, probably Tom's brother coming back with a client.

Finally, Michael gathered his courage and asked, "What condition? Now that you told me half of the story, you may as well tell me the rest."

Tom tilted his head and stared at Michael long and hard. "You never got my message, did you?"

What was to come would be important. He shook his head slowly, once. "What message?"

"I think you better sit down again," Tom said quietly, pointing to the armchair in front of his desk.

Michael waited a bit, but then took the chair hesitantly. He positioned himself comfortably, took a heavy breath, and fixated on Tom expectantly, who also returned to his earlier position, crossing his legs. Tom folded his hands, looked down and pondered how to begin the conversation.

"Okay, Tom. Give it to me. What have I missed?" Michael's eyes dug deeper into Tom, still not understanding fully what was to come.

"Michael, listen, what I am about to tell you does not come from me." Tom glanced up, narrowing his eyes directly at his old friend. "Basically, it may not leave this room. It did not come from my mouth. You need to promise me this."

Michael watched, emotionless, wondering what to expect. "Whatever Tom, a promise from one convict to another," Michael said dryly without changing expression. He did not expect any comment.

Tom scratched his cheek, not sure how to continue. "You want a coffee?"

"As long as you continue talking."

Tom relaxed a bit and hit a button on a large telephone on the table. "Two coffees, please, Mary, usual for me and a jar of milk and some sugar, in case our guest wishes to help himself." He heard a click and Tom sat back. You could hear an expresso machine roar behind the door. They both sat there in silence, listening to the percolation, while Michael really wanted Tom to continue talking.

To Michaels relief, Tom finally opened his mouth and blurted out, "You know why Mayor Hayden was so upset?"

Initially Michael did not know what to do with the statement. Neither did Tom continue, and another wordless moment reigned. Suddenly the door opened, without a knock, and Mary walked in with a tray. She placed everything neatly on the table and disappeared. Michael was so busy with the intake of the last words he had heard that he did not even bother to look at her. Then he blinked and time stopped. The last words of Tom just hung in the air in front of him. *Mayor Hayden.*

"Did you just say *Hayden*?"

"Yes, Mayor Hayden, do you know him?" Tom said expectantly.

Michael blinked again, took a deep breath, closed his eyes, and let out a long exhalation, closing his mouth and blowing up his cheeks. A knot formed in his stomach. At first small, then it grew as if a balloon was pumped up inside. A few seconds passed and it popped. He threw his head back and looked at the ceiling, placing his hands on the side rail of his chair.

"Feeling okay, Michael? Have your coffee." Tom took his cup, which obviously had already been prepared, and pushed everything else towards his guest.

Michael opened his eyes and looked at his coffee, biting his lips. He leaned forward, took the milk with slightly shaking hands, and added it to his coffee, almost overfilling it. He continued with the sugar and put in two spoons, stirred carefully, and placed it on the saucer, after clinking it on the top of his cup to let the last drop fall from the spoon.

Tom took a slow sip while watching Michael, who leaned back with his cup in one hand and holding the saucer with the other. "There is something you know, don't you?"

Michael slowly shook his head in disbelief. "I visited the grave yesterday morning, the grave of Flynn Meier."

He remembered the names on the headstone, *Marta and George Hayden*. So, it was probably someone very close to the mayor that had been killed that very night. Now it was not a stretch for him to understand why Judge Carter had been so harsh and why he pressed for such a high sentence. Perhaps that was the answer to the riddle. It was at least a strong feeling that he had.

"Well, I am impressed. You have figured it out yourself, almost at least. You did not know though that the mayor's name was Hayden, did you? I did not tell you in prison."

"I only just got to town twenty-six years ago, and then I was gone. I was not much into politics, really. Who cares about who the mayor is? He has a different name. There was no connection, so I doubt I would have figured it out any earlier, anyway. But do not hold back, Tom." Michael sipped at his coffee and wanted to listen to the rest of the story now.

"Anyway, people talk, and people watch. He obviously had his people on the inside of the prison. I do not know who, but it could have been anybody. In any case, I was known to be your chess partner."

"OK. So, what."

"Well, that is what I thought initially, so what. It only became an issue when I started here, and my brother wanted that stretch of land." Tom paused. "Look Michael, you need to promise me this," Tom said in a low voice, "this must not leave this room. This could be ..."

"Okay, yes, you had already said it, please, just continue," Michael interrupted, "you owe me this."

Tom took a few more sips and Michael followed.

"Michael, what I am trying to say ... it was the deal. I stay away from you, I will not contact you, and in exchange I get the land. Free of charge, of course. To be exact, a free lease. It is still owned by the commune and guess who controls it."

"The mayor?"

"Indirectly, but yes. The land is publicly owned, so they can do with it what they want. The mayor had the prison built and had control of all the lands in the whole region. Before I got out, my brother was in the application for this terrain. One day, this person came and presented himself as someone from the commune. He took a long walk with my brother. Two weeks later when I was out, the same walk was taken, but just him and me, my brother following clearly behind me. I had the choice, and it was not really an option, as you can understand. Even if I had not accepted and my brother neither, they would have come up with something else, probably, to stop me."

"Any record of this deal?"

"You must be kidding. This deal went so smoothly for my brother, you cannot imagine. They called it, 'Development of infrastructure to enhance local employment.' My brother needed to hire two more people to manage the extra business. The terrain was evenly tarred, free of charge. Commune had people working here for months. Nice employment publicity, people who look for jobs are hired and are paid to work. The mayor was going for his next term, so he needed the publicity. He even boasted about it publicly that he gets jobs for the people. 'Just vote me,' he kept yelling. 'Jobs, jobs, jobs, I will provide them.' Well, he gave the public this example, so you can imagine the positive publicity he got. But nobody asked how much we paid for this, not a single soul."

"So, this is somehow yours now, for the deal."

"This was the clever part. It is a one-hundred-year lease, free of charge. It says so on the signed paper. The cause was nominated exactly as I have just said, 'Development of infrastructure.'"

"Very smart, so he has you in his hands. He could probably cancel the lease at any moment, the cause being something like state repossession. Just build a public parking lot, probably the easiest of all."

"Michael, I had no choice but to accept. My back was against the wall. You have no idea how powerful all these connections are."

"I do, I assure you, I do. I lived it." Michael looked out of the window and back at Tom. "What is this old bastard doing today?"

"Well, old and retired, but still powerful, powerful enough indeed to revoke the lease. He ran many terms, was almost a self-runner, no opposition, too popular to upset anyone. He had and still has a lot of connections."

Michael drained his cup and placed it with the saucer on the tray. "Please continue."

"Well, there is not much more to it." Tom also finished his cup but held on to it. "I know this is hard, and I am sorry. In fact, it does not matter what I say. Look, I had no choice."

Michael licked his upper lip and gazed out of the window once more. *What now?* he asked himself. *What shall I do with this information?* He looked back at Tom. "Any idea how the Mayor Hayden and Judge Carter are related?"

"Judge who? Never heard of him." Tom shook his head and pushed up his lower lip. "Sorry, the name does not ring a bell."

"I thought you were a lawyer; you must know everyone in the judicial system."

"Almost, but I was a lawyer in family matters, specialized in family law. Issues I had to do with were divorces, child custody support, parenting time, wills, or trusts. Whoever it is you just mentioned, I have never heard of him."

"Okay, never mind. In any case, I am a bit cleverer now." Michael paused again and was thinking how to best formulate his next words. "Tom, I do not know if you remember that very last day when we had this strange conversation. You whispered all these things about the prison being a *Pilot Project.* Do you remember that conversation we had on your final day? You promised me you would do some digging."

"Well, as I said, I was stopped."

"So how did you make this connection then? The mayor and Flynn Meier do not have the same surname."

"Clever question, you are smart," Tom said, smiling and nodding his head. "I didn't at first. But I figured it out. I decided to investigate a bit but not too much. I was certainly intrigued and thought, why the hell can't I see you in prison? What is so special about you and then it dawned, you were also the person who had received such as a strange long sentence."

"And how did you find out?"

"It was not difficult; I did one plus one. I checked the funeral records, it is public. All I had to do was to check the newspaper articles in the public library. Go and look at them yourself if you want. The funeral was during your trial. Find the funeral record, look at the date, find the daily local gazette, there are a few, and all of them reported it. Front page, big picture, the mayor and his wife, mourning at the cemetery. Your case did not go unnoticed. I asked myself simply why the mayor and his wife would be in black, at the front of the congregation, mourning?"

"So, there was a funeral while my case was being discussed."

Michael shook his head. *Why didn't Vincent, that bloody good for nothing lawyer say anything?* He tried to put all the information into compartments. It was all becoming too much to handle.

Tom kept watching Michael and did not want to continue. He wanted Michael to pose the questions. It was uncomfortable for him to keep talking. After all, it was true: he let him down.

"Okay Tom, the public library it is then. It is there I can find the record?"

"Yes, easy to find, end of High Street, junction to the main park. How are you here?"

"I got dropped off."

"I can take you, if you want."

"No, thanks, I assume there is public transport?"

"Uh, I am not sure, hang on, let me check."

Tom hit the big button on the big phone again and asked, "Mary, tell me, what buses go to High Street?"

"Number eight, five or six stops."

Tom released the button without thanking the secretary. "Okay, so just behind the exit of this building to the right is the bus station. Buses tend to run frequently. I see them often passing by. Are you sure you do not want a ride?"

"Yes, I prefer to take the bus. Gives me time to think."

"As you wish. Well, let me walk you to the door."

Tom stood up and opened his right-hand drawer and took out a black case. "Here a small gift from me, courtesy of Banes Automobile."

Michael remained motionless, looking up at Tom. "Just one last question. You never told me what message you tried to send me."

Tom breathed in, blinked, and looked at his gift. "Just one sentence. 'Cannot visit, order from the outside. Something is up. KE2.'"

"King to E2."

"I knew you would understand that it was me. I sent it anonymously. I could not have risked being linked to the letter. But obviously you never got it. I am sorry."

Michael watched, unmoved. *Same as Vincent then. Another letter that never arrived.*

"Here Michael, please take it."

Michael stood up and took a small heavy black box from Tom with his right hand and looked at it. "What is it?"

"Nothing special. A gift we give, though only to our best customers. It is something utilized during celebrations."

Michael took it without a word and decided to open it later. He put it into the pocket of his coat and realized he had not even taken it off during his whole stay. Finally, he thought that it would be better to say something. *Just stay polite*, he said to himself. "Thanks, I will check it tonight."

Tom walked Michael out across the huge car dealership, and they said goodbye at the exit.

"Do drop by again, will you? Maybe for a game of chess?" Tom said casually, tapping Michael on the shoulder as a parting gesture.

"Do you still play?" Michael responded.

"No, I have to admit. There is somehow less time now. Strange, this thing about time, isn't it? When you have plenty of it you try to be tremendously organized to ensure you use it well, like during prison time; you are disciplined, and you are particularly good at planning. Once I was out though, I found that I never had time for anything anymore. Life is so fast now, believe me, sometimes I wonder whether it was better when I was locked away. I was able to relax, do things I really liked and most importantly, I was never stressed. Days now run by in the blink of an eye. Before you realize it, the week or the month is gone. It was exactly one week ago that I stood here, seeing off an old client. His name was also Michael, what a coincidence. He said that he is considering selling all he has. Taking the money and donating it."

"Did he tell you why?"

"He had told me he would keep enough cash for a flight to Bhutan in the Himalayas and then live as a Buddhist monk there. You know, he said exactly what I just told you? Time is running too fast when you are in this modern world. You have time for nothing, as you do so much that you do not even have a moment to reflect anymore. You get up and before you realize it, you are already in bed and the whole damn cycle repeats itself when you wake up. You know how long I am out?"

"Of course. I was in for twenty-six years. You left after ten years. So, the law of math says it is sixteen years."

"Sixteen bloody years. Would you believe me that these years passed quicker than my ten in prison?"

"No, I cannot really imagine. How can this be possible?"

"Michael, sixteen years, and what have I achieved? I am stressed, fell out with my sweet daughter that once called me daddy, divorced my wife. I have headaches, back pain and I grew a bit too much, becoming overweight. I was in perfect condition when I came out. I was a happy guy at the time. I had no worries."

Divorced your wife. So that is why you are seeing that secretary with the tight skirt. Michael decided not to say it.

"Make sure you make the most of it, now that you are out, Michael. But take my advice: do not try to do all and everything that is possible in the future. And most of all, do keep away from the social media. It kills you. It makes you stay on the ball twenty-four hours a day. You never have any peace because you cannot switch off. That is why my last sixteen years were hell. There may be a moment you will regret to be free again."

CHAPTER 17

The Library

They shook hands and after they had said goodbye, Michael stood in silence at the bus station in his usual pensive mood. He reflected and pondered on the parting conversation he had with Tom, about life running away so quickly. He saw a girl crossing the street, while she was tapping away on her phone. She did not even bother to look out for traffic. Another young lad was standing next to him, also typing away on his device. Next to him another person was doing the same. He actually did not see anybody who was not looking down and occupied with their device.

Jack had explained to him the meaning of social media one evening on the patio. He looked at the cars passing by. Most drivers were holding their phones to their ear, chatting away. Michael was the only one standing still with his hands in his pockets. *Must be pretty busy, all these people.* He thought about his final exam at university and also how busy he was, as time flew by. The three-hour exam paper went by in a split second. In prison though, three hours felt like an eternity. "Everything is relative," Albert Einstein said once.

Finally, he saw an orange bus arriving, which stopped sharply at the terminal. It had the number eight written on a display at the front. He hopped on, paid a single note, and took a seat at the front, diagonally behind the bus driver. Riding along, he watched the driver maneuver confidently onto the street. He repassed the whole conversation he had with Tom Bane. Michael felt even more betrayed by the world than before. So many people were involved; he was just the victim. Vincent disappeared, Tom disappeared, the judge was a mystery and now the mayor. What was his involvement? There must be something, Tom had indicated. *What is the relationship between Mayor Hayden and Flynn Meier? How did Judge Carter get involved?* These are the two questions Michael kept repeating as the bus stopped and took on passengers, while others got out. He looked at the electronic display to check on upcoming bus-stations above him, craning his neck. *Three more stops.*

Like a bolt of lightning, one sentence of Tom's flashed back to him. "People talk, and people watch. He obviously had his people on the inside of the prison." So, it meant someone was spying on him in prison. "I do not know who," Tom had said. Michael started sweating. *Had Jack deceived me, is he the mole?* He was confused. Was Jack just putting him up to keep an eye on him? But that seemed impossible, otherwise why would he point him in all directions to find the clues? He was not sure what to think but was sure that he wanted to confront Jack tonight.

"High street," came the speaker's voice.

"Excuse me sir," he addressed the driver. "To get to the library, do I need to get off here?"

"Next stop is better, less to walk. You just need to walk back a little bit."

"Thank you, sir, in this case I get off here and keep on going in the same direction."

"Absolutely. I guess about ten minutes. Button up, it is frisky outside. Have a nice day." The driver smiled at him and waited until his passenger got out, Michael waving back at the driver, thanking him loudly. He felt good to have had a polite short exchange with the driver. He realized that if you are nice, others are nice. In prison all conversations had a hint of mistrust. The laws in confinement were different. If you were too friendly, somebody often took advantage of you.

He saw the bus rush by and headed in the same direction, passing shop after shop. He wondered why people needed so much stuff. He passed at least four shoe boutiques and gazed at the assortment. He had one pair, with thick soles, which was enough for the season. For the summer he may buy himself another pair.

He had almost passed the library but realized in time that there was a building with a long set of stairs on the other side of the street. He crossed and stepped up on the long flight. When he entered through a set of double doors, he found himself in a large hall. In front of him he saw a thick rectangular metal frame placed upright, with two security officers standing around, chatting away. Next to the metal frame was a horizontal belt, which disappeared into a big metal box. The last time Michael had seen this was at the airport when he flew to New York.

"Good morning, sir," one of the officers greeted him, smiling. "If you have any objects on you, please place them on the belt and then you can walk through this gate, please."

Michael nodded, lifted his hands without responding and walked through the rectangular frame, which then beeped loudly. Surprised, he spun around.

"Sorry sir, I need to frisk you."

"Of course, I understand."

He was patted expertly around arms and legs. Michael felt a shiver and had a flashback to twenty-six years ago when he was last body-searched, the day he had entered the prison. He shook slightly at the thought.

The officer looked at him in a friendly manner, "All okay, sir?"

"Sure, yes, I am just a bit sensitive."

"Could you please take off your coat and lay it on the belt, please, I think there is something in your pocket."

Then he remembered, he had actually totally forgotten the gift of Tom. "Of course, officer, I think it is something a friend just gave me."

"No worries, just take it out, please, and put it on the belt together with your coat. Then please walk again back through the security check."

He slipped off his coat and walked back through the gate again, which beeped. He took out the package that Tom gave him, and laid it on the belt, together with the coat. He wondered what that heavy thing was. He repassed the gate and the security officer, one hand on his revolver, who smiled as the gate lit up all green without emitting a sound. Michael wondered what happened to this world that you are controlled like this. He assumed this was just a simple library where you go to get a book.

"Sir, would you mind opening this box, please?" another officer, sitting in a chair staring into a huge screen, said to him.

Michael took his coat and put it on, then opened the black box carefully, as one of the officers stepped by closely to see what he was unpacking. He slid out a heavy metal object that reminded him of a big pocketknife. It seemed to have a corkscrew attached to one side and on the other side there was a huge blade, which could be unfolded. A big inscription was on the surface of the spine: *Banes*.

"Sir, you are not allowed to take this inside. You can place it in this plastic box, and when you leave you may take it again. Are you okay with this?" the officer said sternly as he pointed to a table with a green box.

"Certainly, officer," Michael replied. *Thanks for getting me into trouble, Tom*, he thought to himself.

The library was empty. It was two in the afternoon. Probably most people were at work, children at school and students at university. Just the unemployed or pensioners were wandering around at this time of day. He saw a lady with glasses wearing a cardigan and walking around with a clipboard. He guessed she worked there.

"Excuse me, maybe you can help me."

"Of course, how may I assist you?"

"I wonder if I am able to see the newspaper editions of the main town gazette of about twenty-six years back."

"Yes, no problem. First floor, ask for Mrs. Frey."

"So, you kept all the newspapers for such a long time?"

"Oh, no. It is now all digitalized."

There was that word again. *Digital*. Michael raised his eyebrows and nodded as if he understood what she meant. Then he remembered what Jack had explained when he spoke about his video tapes of New York. *All digital today.* "Oh, so it is on the computer now, I assume?"

"Yes, absolutely right, the newspapers were all scanned a few years back, and you can see all editions now on the online portal of the town's library, first floor, ask for Mrs. Frey."

Michael took the stairs, slowly, feeling quite proud of himself for having understood everything. He managed to hold a conversation about computers. He smiled and was quite satisfied with his progress. *Online*, he guessed that also meant computer. He was not so sure what the difference was between *online* and *digital* but understood that both had to do with the computer.

On the first floor he saw another lady with a stack of books passing by, whom he followed swiftly. As she put them away on a shelf, she eyed him.

"Hello sir, may I help you?"

"Yes, please, could you kindly show me where I may view the newspaper editions of twenty-six years ago? That are now online?" he quickly added, confidently.

"Certainly, just come with me. It is here, on the grey computer. The first one on the left," she said, walking into the left-hand corner of the room.

There were four computers situated next to each other and she pointed to the corner computer. Above on the wall was written, *Historical scans*.

"You see, this one we use to save all the scans we have done over the years, just for archiving. It has no Internet access. Please have a seat and move the mouse and then you can see a simple menu. Just click on *newspaper* and type in the year, month and date."

Michael sat down, moved the mouse and a menu appeared. On it was the word *Local Gazette*. After clicking on it, he saw eight spaces, requesting the input of the day, month, and year. It had been a long time since he handled a computer, but these were functions you do not forget. *It's like driving a car*, he thought to himself.

"That's it, if you need me, just give me a call. There are not so many people here at the moment, so I have some time to spare. You will find me over there," Mrs. Frey smiled and pointed into the opposite corner of the room where he saw a big trolley with the words *return books* written across.

He breathed deeply. *Okay let's go Michael. You can do it.* He calculated, reflected hard, and remembered the burial of Flynn Meier on the cemetery cross as the 28th of February. *Or was it earlier?* He was not sure. Possible newspaper article on the 1st of March 1996. "Okay, let's try." He typed in the date and hit enter. He saw the front page of the *Gazette* and read about politics, sports, and celebrities. But nothing about a local town issue. *Let's go back.* He entered the 28th of February and read. He saw nothing. He continued further back to the 25th, nothing. He sat back incredulously. "That is not possible," he said loudly. 2nd of March, nothing, 3rd of March, nothing. Then he got a hit on the 4th of March.

Michael Fletcher is now incarcerated and condemned to serve his sentence in our penitentiary. He entered yesterday, after the verdict.

There was a big black and white picture of him in handcuffs guided away by an officer. He felt a shiver running down his back. He decided not to go further, as he knew the rest. There was nobody better than him who knew what went on. *But where is the missing funeral report?* It is the question he repeated in his head several times. He went through the sequence a couple times again, starting from the 25th and arriving at the 28th. Then it dawned.

"Well, that must be it. Let's try it," he said to the computer. He typed the 29th of February 1996. *Bingo, a leap year.* He almost smiled. The newspaper of the *Local Gazette* came up and a big photo was depicted on the front page. People mourning and two middle aged people were right in the front row at the grave, both dressed in black, the woman completely veiled.

Michael sat back and remembered again what Tom had said about the funeral photo. His stomach flipped as he looked at the picture again. Everyone there in that picture must have given him the blame. When this picture was taken he was at trial, blamed for the death of that person being buried. He decided to read the article that followed.

After a tragic incident Flynn Meier found his resting place in the family grave, beside his grandparents. He passed away young and innocent. Jane and Mayor John Hayden attended the funeral and showed great grief after having mourned for fourteen days. The congregation of one hundred people showed their respect.

Michael decided to stop. He did not want to know more. He saw Flynn's grave, which was enough for him. He did this search not to read the full burial report. There was something else that intrigued him now. Where was the connection? Flynn Meier was buried in the family grave among his grandparents. However, he had a different family name. What was the direct relationship between the mayor and Flynn? He got up and went to Mrs. Frey.

"Oh, hello, sir, got all you needed?"

"Yes, thank you. I was wondering if I was able to do a search on the Internet?"

"Certainly, let me set you up, there is a short procedure, for which I need your ID, I assume you have it on you. It does not take longer than a few seconds."

Michael followed the librarian and took it out of his inside pocket. It was renewed the day before he had left prison. It was brand new.

The librarian went to the computer to the right of the one which he used before. However, then she moved again left, quickly, to the first one. "You need to click on the X here, to close the session you were working on, otherwise someone can see what you had searched." She took the mouse and closed the window. Michael nodded simply. "So, please sit down and put your ID on the scanner here on the right." He made himself comfortable and did as he was told. "Now smile and look into that camera."

Unsure why he had to have his picture taken he followed suit, as Mrs. Frey held a blue chip in her hand attached to a retractable key ring that was fixed to her belt. She extended it and held it against a box attached to the scanner.

"Now please click on *OK*, here." Michael followed the instruction and looked at her, unsure what to say.

"Now let me explain. You just consented to the data privacy record. The scan of your ID and the picture which we took will be saved for 72 hours. Then it will be cancelled automatically. Any misuse of the Internet is reported to us usually within 24 hours. You cannot imagine how much nuisance people engage in on the web. We have had so many bad experiences we had to put in this measure, to trace back to anybody who misused access. Any security measures or firewalls have not been successful. So, we tell the users that we can find them should they do anything inappropriate."

"Fine Mrs. Frey, I understand," he said with a trace of regret. He had not understood a word. *What is a firewall, or in any case, what can I do that is inappropriate?* Maybe he would ask Jack later to explain this to him.

"Enjoy, and this service is of course free of charge. You can use it as long as you wish." The librarian double-clicked on a symbol, smiled again at Michael, and then left.

Michael had watched Jack the last few days and got an idea of what to do. He immediately placed the mouse on the search bar and typed, *Flynn Meier and John Hayden*. A long list of article links came up on the screen. He wiped his mouth and chin and then clicked on the first link.

He read article after article about the work of the Mayor John Hayden. Several articles were also written on the death of Flynn Meier and his work as an owner of the casino, but nothing really connecting the two. Mayor

Hayden had an exceptionally long career as a mayor, having been reelected many times. Numerous pictures and events were displayed. The last mention of Flynn Meier was his burial.

Michael sat back and thought. He was getting tired, as he was certainly not used to working for such long periods. The computer screen also strained his eyes. He closed them and decided to rest, to recollect himself.

The heating and air conditioning system was in slow mode and emitted a humming and whining noise above him. The computer was buzzing slightly. He hadn't slept so badly the previous night, but a feeling of drowsiness crept over him. After a while he then reopened his eyes, leaned forwards, and typed, *Flynn Meier father*. New links came up, but again with no real clues. There seemed to be many Flynn Meiers in the world. He tried another search by typing the four words: *mayor John Hayden son*.

Michael shook his head in disbelief. There it stood: *Jane and John Hayden adopt boy*. He clicked and it confirmed what he had expected.

Jane and John Hayden have decided to give Flynn Meier a home in their family. Flynn Meier, eight years old, had lost his parents in a tragic accident. Jane and John do not have children. The boy will retain his family name, in remembrance of his parents and will be now officially the legal son of Mayor John and Jane Hayden.

He saw a picture of a younger John Hayden and a younger boy together with a woman who must be Jane Hayden, probably the same person who was veiled.

Michael sat back and rubbed his eyes. He really had to put this together correctly. Flynn Meier was the adopted son of Mayor Hayden. Tom had talked of someone powerful he had upset. Was this him? It is a question that now circled his mind. And then there was also the bribe, the one that Tom and his brother accepted to receive the parking lot. Vincent, his lawyer, likewise disappeared, possibly also influenced by the decision of the mayor. Piece by piece he started to connect the dots.

Michael continued to sit there for a while. He felt drained and tired, but mainly betrayed. Was really the cause for his long sentence–the pressure exerted by the mayor? How was this possible? He must have surely influenced the judge. He wondered how it was possible to influence the judge to such an extent.

He decided to get up and leave but held on for a moment. He took the mouse and closed the window. He did not want Mrs. Frey telling him off again. He walked across the floor as the librarian appeared.

"Thank you, I have finished."

"Thank you for coming. Did you log out?"

"I pressed the X to close the window."

She smiled and said, "Well, it may not have been enough, but don't worry, I will take care to check. Have a nice day."

Michael wondered again what she meant, but then recalled that he also had to log out when he was at university. Next time he would do better. He walked down the stairs and saw the smiling officers again who were busy chatting away. When one of them saw him, he walked across to the green box and took the present of Tom and handed it to him.

"Here you are, sir," he grinned, "have a nice day."

"Thank you, officer, same to you." Michael left, walking outside down the flight of stairs.

It was a dull and windless afternoon. He turned up the collar of his coat, looked left and right, then headed for the approximate direction where he believed Jack lived. He was proud of what he had achieved, on his own, doing research in the modern world. You are never too old to learn, was something he always told his students in prison.

At that moment memories came back, Michael remembered Joey well; he was in his late forties and had already served five years. He got himself ten years for killing somebody involuntarily while drunk. As Michael plowed along, teaching Fernando all the basics of algebra, Joey sat patiently next to Michael for many months. He was allowed to participate. This spared him time in isolation in his cell. A privilege given to anybody willing to study and learn with Michael. Not only was prison promoting finishing school, but study was also regarded as valuable education for the time after release. "I never understood math and I will never will," Joey said after the first sessions, watching Fernando apply all that Michael taught him. However, Joey kept coming to the lessons for months, which became years, to save him from time in isolation. But after some time of participation Joey started to solve questions that he never dreamt he would. It was one day, years later, when Michael received a letter, one of a very few, addressed to him personally. It was from Joey.

Dear Michael, my old friend, I do not know how to thank you, but I managed to get a job at a mechanical store. I am now looking after the accounts, thanks to the mathematical skills you taught me. Thank you for all you did. Yours, Joey.

Michael had every right to be proud. Joey not only finished school, but also got a job, thanks to him.

Jack lived somewhere on the western fringe of town, so he knew he had to simply walk in that direction. It would be a long walk of about two hours, he guessed, but he needed this time to clear his head. He had seen all the people so far connected to the case, even Eileen, the witness. He wondered if it made sense after all to see the mayor. But he had already discussed this with Jack. What was there to say? *Hello, I am sorry, but why did you ask Judge Carter to give me such a long sentence?* Likely a stupid question to ask. After so many years, could a case be made against him for influencing a judge? What was he to gain? He was not sure. As he walked the streets, he tried to orient himself and continued to walk in the direction of Jack's house. A few things were still not clear to him, though. Who was the spy in prison, and who, most importantly, was the jogger? But finding him would be a hopeless task. He had absolutely no clues to follow and the only witness, Eileen, was not able to provide any further information.

He continued to march along and soon arrived at the house of his current stay. The neighborhood changed and less cars circulated. It was getting late. He wondered how he would approach his discussion with Jack. Jack was surely curious about everything that had happened today. However, Michael had something else in the back of his mind. Two crucial questions hung densely, and he wondered how to affront Jack with these. Two things that Jack possibly was related to. Should he accuse him directly or was he supposed to be more prudent and ask for his opinion? He was not sure.

CHAPTER 18

The Accusation

Jack sat outside on the patio reading a newspaper when Michael arrived and was greeted by a big grin. A few flies were buzzing around his head, attracted by a lamp that beamed from above. "Well, old scout, I see you found your way!"

Michael stepped onto the patio and took a chair, a bit tired. "Quite a walk from the library, I can tell you. I made some interesting discoveries."

"Well, I guessed you did not come walking here from the dealership. You may have taken a bus for some of the distance. But why the library?"

Michael was not sure where to start and pondered. Then he got up again and said, "Come, let us go for a stroll."

"Are you sure? You look tired."

"Sure, I can talk and think better when I am walking."

"Off we go then, whatever you say."

They headed down the street into the darkening sky. Michael was about to begin the story with the visit to Tom, but there was the first burning question he had to simply relieve himself of first. So, without further hesitation he fixed his eyes on Jack and simply blurted out, "Did you know they intercepted my letters?"

Jack ignored the stare and kept walking at the same rate, not reacting to the question promptly. Michael felt from his lack of immediate response that Jack was trying to formulate a suitable answer.

Jack then stopped, took out his hands and spread his arms. "Don't look at me this way. I swear I had nothing to do with this."

Michael looked down and continued to walk. It was chilly and he started to shiver. Winter and spring were still taking their turns these days, the winter still dominating the evenings. Whether, though, it was really from the cold or the agitation and rage, he was not sure. Jack watched him move on and then followed, picking up pace.

"Michael, I was not on any day shift. Only in the daytime did the letters arrive. I have not seen a single one."

"And how did you know, then?" His voice became scratchy.

"As I said, I was running only nightshift. Post only arrived on days. Yes, I was told about these instructions but had not seen any. The instructions were verbal, so no traces. All letters are opened and checked, that is a rule in prison, to avoid smuggling of illegal substances. You cannot imagine all the stuff that arrives, hidden between two pieces of paper."

"What were these instructions?"

Jack took a deep breath while trying to keep up with the pace of walking. "Any letter for you must be checked and passed by the warden. I have no idea what he was asked to do or by whom he was asked. I guess he decided what you would get."

"Carry on."

"I was advised by *The Law*; you remember the warden. When I started work the very first week, he told me to watch out for any mail or message to you. I was not allowed to pass them on but was to give it to him. He said specifically that he was given the order to inspect them personally. When I hesitated to better understand what he meant, and I remember that very expression on his face, he said the following to me, and I will never forget these words: 'You have only started this week. Better stick to what I tell you to do.' He looked at me sternly and said one last sentence, before patting my shoulder, 'Remember what I just said, you have a long way to go here.' I was still new on the job at the time and was rather intimidated."

After a few more steps Michael said in a flat and calm fashion. "So, you knew they opened my letters and checked that there were no hidden or prohibited contents side. I guess they were all read. Just mine or also those of others?"

"Possibly just yours, maybe also others, but yours for sure."

Michael stopped walking. "Why didn't you tell me?"

Jack stopped as well and turned around slowly to face Michael. "Look, I am sorry, you are just out, and this is the first time we are having this conversation. I could have hardly told you inside."

"Why not?"

"Because you would have complained."

"Of course, I would have."

"And I would have lost my job."

"Nobody would have known it was you."

"Of course, they would have, by elimination."

"By elimination?"

"Those on the day shift stick together. They would have ruled out each other. I would have been the only one left. Very simple."

Michael walked on and Jack followed. "So, any important letter or message was then intercepted."

"That was the message passed, and therefore probably also the reason why you never got post from Vincent."

"Well, I can tell you, from Tom, also!" Michael stopped again and looked at Jack.

"Tom also sent you messages," Jack said in blank manner, "that I was absolutely not aware of. He told you this today?"

It was getting dark, but Michael still saw his face fully. There was something in his gaze that did not convince him. He pondered on his next question and contemplated again how directly he should shoot the question at his presumed friend.

"Michael, I can see there is something else really bothering you. Go ahead, spit it out. No use procrastinating now." Jack picked up the pace again while Michael remained immobile, watching as Jack walked away.

Then he shouted, loudly, "Be honest, did you spy on me?"

Jack spun round and looked hurt. "What do you mean by that?"

Michael strode on and faced Jack. "Because there was someone keeping watch on me, or whoever I dealt with."

"How do you know this, now?"

"Also, Tom told me this. He said that there was someone on the inside reporting what I did and with whom I was with."

"How does Tom know all this?"

Michael told him what happened at the dealership, his discussion with Tom and what happened to him, missing out the part about the bribe for the car park. He had promised this to Tom.

"So, Tom was told by some mysterious guy to stay away from you? He was not allowed to visit, and you never received his messages. Now that is interesting, indeed."

"It is indeed." Michael looked at Jack expectantly, wanting him to continue.

"I admit to having known about the letter, but I was absolutely not aware of anybody keeping watch on you. How could I, I was a single man doing shifts during the sleeping hours."

Michael was unsure what to make of this conversation he just had. Was Jack being very honest to him and had absolutely nothing to do with the abnormalities during his incarceration? It was true, Jack was on night shift only, and what was there to report about him. He was in his cell and did nothing else during these hours.

A minute or so passed, during which neither found anything to say, then Jack finally broke the silence. "You haven't yet told me what you did at the library."

"No, I haven't." Michael was not in a mood to speak about it. He was upset.

They continued walking when Jack turned to Michael. "Are we good, after this little tiff between two friends?"

Michael did not know how to respond; he was still cross with Jack.

"Maybe I should have been more honest to you. I am sorry, Michael, I should have told you about the issue of the letters at once a few days ago, when you discovered that those of Vincent had not been passed on to you."

"That's okay," Michael responded, with a hint of sarcasm. "I have become used to being the victim. That is the way life works. Some take all the blame and when you can shuffle more onto somebody who has already been found guilty, less shit sticks on the others. Give the scapegoat all he can carry. It is life in the modern world, isn't it?"

Jack paused briefly but then said, "You might have a point here. In this modern age, Michael, I regret to admit, that the weakest link always falls behind. People have become adept at exploiting such circumstances."

They continued walking and Jack noticed Michael was shivering. "Let's go home and sit inside, then you can tell me what you did at the library. It is rather chilly now and you have been out in the open for some time."

As they settled down at home, Jack came with two steaming cups of chamomile tea.

"This will warm you up a bit. It has also got healing properties, a fairly good drink against anxieties, makes you also sleep better." He placed them on the table and Michael sat down, thanking him. "So, I am all ears, what did you do at the library?"

Michael took the cup and warmed his hands. It felt good. He wasn't accustomed to enduring prolonged exposure to cold temperatures.

"Where shall I start. I told you what Tom had said about trying to do some digging. He did actually. He never managed to pass any message to me though. He was intrigued why I had received such a long sentence. When he was out, he checked the funeral records and the report on the funeral itself. There is a big photo of the same place we stood yesterday." Michael looked expectantly at Jack to check for a reaction. Jack showed his poker face as usual, so Michael continued. "Well, guess what, the mayor and his wife, standing right there at the front in black, mourning. And guess what, there is Hayden. Rings a bell, doesn't it? Hayden? Same inscription on the headstone as the one where Flynn Meier is buried."

"That is what you found in the library?"

"Yes, after the hint from Tom. And not only that. I searched up both names. Flynn's and the mayor's. They are related. The mayor adopted Flynn many years back and it explains why the mayor was at the front, mourning. Now I did not need to do one plus one anymore. It is pretty obvious."

"Tell me." Jack took his cup and blew into it, steam covering his face.

"Well, it is obvious, Jack. I was made to suffer. As I took the wrath of the mayor, he did everything in his power to make my stay as long as possible, as I killed his legal son; and he stuck me into that prison which he controlled to keep an eye on me."

"Well, I have to say, you make a good detective, even a better one than I have been. I am impressed," Jack responded nonchalantly.

Michael looked at Jack and he felt that something was amiss. Jack had not reacted as usual. He knew something he didn't but decided not to dwell upon it further. It was as if Jack already knew everything he had just been told.

"What I am very curious to know is what relationship there is between the judge and the mayor. This lengthy sentence of mine and also my stay in that particular prison, it seems that there was some influence by the mayor. But how the hell did he convince the judge?"

"What did I say last time? Step on his feet. Go and see him. He may make a wrong move and say something he did not mean to. You are definitely on the right track."

"I want to go tomorrow. Perhaps he will be at the park again. People do not change their habits."

"Drink your tea, it is nice and hot. I added a few spoons of honey as well. It is good for your throat. I do not want you to turn ill tonight, after your exposure to the cold today. We do not want to speak to the judge with a blocked nose, do we? He might not understand what you say." Jack did not notice if Michael reacted in any way, but still chuckled as usual at his own joke.

Michael slept well and deeply. The tea had helped him. In the morning though, he fell into an unrestful dream. He was standing in the graveyard. People were hammering away, opening the grave of Flynn Meier. He was moving forward to try to stop them, but they kept battering the tomb. The mayor was standing there and was laughing, pointing at Michael, and next to him was the judge shouting grimly at him as well. He wanted them to stop. He held his ears to stop the noise and was pressing so hard that it hurt. *Don't, please, leave him alone,* he cried. Everyone was laughing, even

Vincent was there looking at him. Suddenly he woke up and was feeling the pain of pressing with his fists on his ears. Then there was the sound again, a continuous hammering, coming from outside on the street. He got up and peeked out of the window. There was roadwork going on and a worker was standing there dressed in a yellow warning vest and an ear muffler. He was leaning heavily on a jackhammer, chiseling into the ground.

He sat there for a while pondering on the significance of his dream. Clearly, he was being haunted by all the people who had betrayed him: the judge, the mayor, Vincent. He did not remember or recognize anybody else in his dream. He was, though, not convinced that there weren't others. He decided not to tell Jack about it. Maybe another time but not now. He had to accomplish several things today. The first was what he had already discussed with Jack, to see the judge again.

CHAPTER 19

The Girl

Jack dropped Michael a few roads prior to the same posh area as he had last time. "I will make my way home on my own again, Jack."

"Very well, the weather is better. Have a great walk then, and good luck. Remember, keep tough today. *I hope you got your long spoon with you,*" Jack voiced, grinning broadly.

Michael looked at him questionably and was not sure what he meant but did not bother to ask. He would do so another time.

When Jack pulled away, Michael started walking. As much as he had marveled last time at the nice houses, this time his mind was elsewhere. He was planning to do two things today. His first mission was to try to talk to the judge again—he hoped to be able to converse more than during his previous encounter. The other he would conduct in the afternoon. How much he was to achieve now was not clear to him. If the judge would not speak, what was he to do? He could not force him and most likely his Honor would never incriminate himself. The cards were not well laid out.

The judge sat, same as last time, on the wooden bench. Michael wondered once more how Jack had known this. He walked across the field, past the playing children, the chatting mothers, and placed himself to the right of the judge. He was again busy, engaged in reading his newspaper. Michael breathed deep and cleared his throat.

His mind rumbled on how to best start his conversation to avoid it ending so rapidly. *Your Honor,* always respectful. He was not going to achieve anything otherwise. He needed these minutes and wanted to stay factual. *Kindly give me these minutes to speak,* would be a polite way to start. *That is a cordial way,* he thought to himself. He felt uneasy, and his chest was tightening. He was nervous and hesitant. Surely, he cannot deny me this. He cleared his throat once more. The judge had not noticed him yet. The last encounter had not gone well, so he needed to remain calmer. He was not going to achieve anything with aggression. Any aggression would only evoke a reaction. He marveled at how science explained the behavior of humanity. He remembered his teacher quoting Newton's third law of physics in his psychology classes. "For every action in nature there is an equal and opposite reaction." He decided to tread carefully. He glanced quicky across and evoked a fake toss to get his attention. He needed to stay diplomatic to make the conversation as long as possible.

"Sorry to bother you again, Your Honor, but please do concede me a few minutes. I mean no harm." Michael looked straight forward, without looking to his left, his hands dug once more very deep in his pockets.

Michael heard a familiar rustling of paper, and the judge looked across at him in horror. "You again, I told you to leave me alone."

"Please, Your Honor, I just want to speak to you for a moment."

"There is absolutely nothing to speak about. I expressed this to you already the last time we had our unpleasant encounter. I will leave at once," he responded and started to get up.

"No, you won't," Michael said in a rising tone. "I understand that the mayor was quite upset."

He let the comment hang in the air. As he expected, the judge did not answer. Instead, he gazed straight ahead and perched forward on the edge of the bench, on the verge of standing up. Then he relaxed and sat back again, placing his paper on his knees and folding his hands on top of it.

"Very well, what do you want to discuss?"

"Why was the mayor so upset?"

"I guess you know the answer yourself, otherwise you would not have mentioned his name." The judge expressed an air of calmness. He was not going to get himself exposed. Michael did not expect him to take part in the conversation. As he just sat there, he realized this. So, he decided to answer his own question.

"We both know it was the mayor's son who was killed, his only son. He must have been devastated. Something you would not even wish on your fiercest enemy." Carter did not react. "Did you meet the mayor sometimes?"

"He is our highest official of the town, or at least he was. He is now retired. But we did convene, as important representatives of this city."

The judge kept himself covered and was not to divulge more than necessary. This Michael was sure of. So why not pose a direct question that had bothered him. "Why did you pass such a severe sentence? It was not second-degree murder. The knife was not even mine. I should have never been judged this way, but you decided not to abide the law!"

"I have no need to give you any explanations. I think the conversation is now over," the judge responded in a belittling manner, as if he were talking to an inferior person.

"On the contrary, actually, this conversation is becoming very interesting indeed. You see, Your Honor, there are some strange coincidences." The judge did not move nor gave any comment. "The mayor's son is killed, I get an extremely high sentence, and I am put into a recently built prison, erected by basically the mayor himself. He even had control over that damn place. Excuse me for the language."

Michael waited and did not hear a single tone. So, he decided to pose the one and only question that had been burning in him for a long time. "Why did you get influenced by the mayor? What does he hold against you?"

He then looked across and wanted to see his reaction. However, the Judge's face bore no expression. "'Will the defendant please rise,' you said to me. Do you know what I felt when you banged the gavel on your desk and condemned me for twenty-six long years?" Michael continued to fixate him.

The judge looked up and turned his head to face Michael. "What do you want?" he snorted.

Michael decided to use his words carefully, took a deep breath and articulated slowly and very clearly. "Did the mayor put you under pressure to pass such a high sentence?"

The judge paused and looked bewildered, raising his head higher in an act of superiority. "Is that a question?"

"You misused your position and were influenced in your decision. I wonder why." Michael pointed his right index finger at him and stood up, facing and towering above him.

The judge looked intensely at Michael, who returned the stare without blinking. "I really have no need at all to continue to converse with you."

They faced each other like two wild animals, watching each other and contemplating what the other would do. "I will find out, mark my word, Your Honor, I will find out, what led you to this decision. There is likely much more to this than I can imagine."

The judge remained calm and indifferent. "Oh, there is really no more to this. You were sentenced, nothing else, rightfully by the law."

"No, I was not, that is the point. First of all, I did not do it, and you know that. Secondly, apart from passing the wrong verdict, you imposed a sentence that did not come from you."

"The verdict was passed by the jury. I asked the jury if they had reached a unanimous decision. It is them who found you guilty, young man, so whether you were guilty or not, you were judged."

"So simple, is it?"

"You can put it the hard way if you want, or you can take my advice, young man."

"That would be, Your Honor?"

"Do not be too inquisitive."

"Why shouldn't I, Your Honor," Michael responded, awaiting an answer. "Anything to hide?"

The judge emitted a derisive grunt. "This is a slanderous nonsense of a detainee who has not accepted his fault. The case was completed a long time past. What are you trying to achieve?"

"What has happened I cannot change. But I can at least find out the truth, which is something you owe me. I was not rightfully judged."

The judge gave him a deprecatory look. "You were judged, as I had already said, rightfully by the law."

"Rightfully? No, it was certainly not, Your Honor, you were influenced, your decision was not based on the law, but on something personal," Michael said in a raised tone, angry but still contained.

The judge looked at Michael, slightly taken aback and controlled, and gave a last contemptuous snort. He took his paper into his right hand, got up looking straight ahead, and started to walk away.

Michael looked to his right and watched him stride off. However, after a few steps, he turned around again and faced Michael once more. "Now leave me alone and never bother me again," Judge Carter spit through gritted teeth. He spun around but after some strides stopped abruptly again.

A well-dressed blonde lady was looking curiously at Judge Carter, waving at him. As Michael continued watching, the judge strode forcefully on. He noticed a furtive wave of hands to the blonde woman, the same way as last time. She was sitting on another park bench. The lady looked up and they exchanged a few words when the judge stopped dead next to her and started articulating with his newspaper. Michael watched the two carefully as their initial moderate exchange turned into a heated conversation. He was sure to have caught the lady glimpsing nervously at him. She passed glances back and forth between him and the judge, becoming increasingly agitated, pointing both of her palms upwards. The exchange continued and then the judge waved and walked off. Michael watched him leave and then he was gone. He pushed his hands back into his pockets and watched the lady intensively. Before he realized it, she was walking slowly towards him. She had an unfriendly air and was small but had a superior gait. She stopped and gazed at him.

"Sir, I believe you are Michael Fletcher, it that so?"

"How do you know me?"

"It is of no importance, really. I would just like to ask you to leave my father alone. He is retired and wants to have nothing to do anymore with his professional life. So kindly refrain from contacting him."

Michael stood there without blinking, wondering why she was getting mixed up in all of this. The woman jerked forward as a little girl ran up behind and bumped into her back, hiding her face deep into her thick winter coat.

"Honey, please go back to your friends, mummy will be along soon." The blonde lady still stared at Michael, almost falling over as the little one kept pushing into her back.

"Mummy, who is this man?" the girl voiced, now grinning behind her back.

"Darling, please go back to the swings. I will be with you in a moment."

Michael looked from the blonde woman down, and then into the face of the little girl who suddenly ditched to the side from behind to look at him. She was small, with long blonde hair. Her face was radiating, sweet and innocent, emitting an aura of peace to Michael. As he contemplated her face his heart leaped. Michael stood there completely mesmerized. He felt a world crushing down on him. It was a sense of déjà vu as he incredulously stared into her eyes. He dug his sight deep into a set of sparkling, shiny blue eyes. They were the same marine blue eyes that had transfixed him for the last twenty-six years.

CHAPTER 20

The Puzzle

As Michael stood there completely startled, the girl smiled broadly at him. He also recognized the same expression that was added to the smile basically two weeks back, after his release, when Jack stood by his car.

"Let's go honey." The blonde lady took her by the hand, and they left walking to the playground, leaving him behind. She glanced once more over her shoulders, expressionless, and then settled with the other mothers after guiding her daughter to her friends again by the swings.

A quite startling resemblance, Michael reflected. The familiarity of her eyes with that of Jack's could surely not be a coincidence. A storm of confusion formed as he tried to digest what he had just realized. Was it really possible that he'd just met Jack's wife and that the judge was his father-in-law? The probability seemed so remote, but at the same time also possible. But why should Jack have then pushed him to come here? He had absolutely no explanation and would have to wait until the evening to confront his presumed new friend. Instead of leaving, he sat down again on the bench with his elbows on his knees, covering his face, hoping to be able to think clearly.

There were just too many coincidences. He had spotted a connection, but it did not make sense. The mayor influencing the judge, Jack pushing Michael to stand on the feet of his father in-law. How was it all related? One thing he was certain of: Jack had a grudge against his father-in-law. He remembered when he asked Jack if he had any family. "Got a small kid, a girl, and fell apart with the family," he recalled well these words, the day he had first entered Jack's house. But surely there was more behind than this.

Michael continued to rest for a while, still pondering, when he finally decided to stand up. He left without looking at the blonde woman, who was already absorbed in deep discussions with her friends. He wanted to risk another glance at those blue eyes, but could not see the little girl, who had mingled among all the playing children somewhere in the playground.

He began to retrace his steps from the park to where Jack had left him, but then remembered of course that his chauffeur had already left and that he would have to make his way home on his own. He looked at the sky to orient himself. The Park was in the eastern, more modern part of the city. He would need to navigate himself west, in the direction of where Jack lived, however, passing the city center where he had other business to deal with. There was indeed something that had to be clarified further now. He strode forcefully in the western direction.

Spring was definitely nearing, and Michael took a few deep breaths of Lent. It was almost warm when the wind stopped, so he decided not to walk too briskly, but simply to enjoy his stroll. The neighborhood changed quickly, from rural to urban houses, less green and more traffic, until he reached a familiar street that he had passed on the bus just the day before. The same bus he had taken, number eight, drove past, so he knew he had to head in the same direction. He walked some more minutes until he arrived at his destination.

He took the same flight of steps he had taken yesterday and was met also by the same officer at the entrance gate nodding with a grin. Michael was glad to have taken out the pocket knife this morning before leaving. He certainly did not want another body search and was relieved to pass freely through the checkpoint. He headed straight up the stairs to the first floor to look for Mrs. Frey, who was casually checking something online, perched in a chair. Michael cleared his throat, "Good day, Mrs. Frey."

She turned around and gave him a welcoming smile. "Oh hello, Mr. Fletcher, was it?"

Michael looked at her for a fraction of a second with a small pain in his chest. He wondered if she recognized his name as someone who had served a prison sentence. After all, the judge had called it a "notorious" case. He wondered generally if people made a connection of his name to a dreadful past incident. She did not seem to react negatively in any way, so relief came just as quickly and the pain in the chest disappeared. "Yes, Mrs. Frey, indeed I am Michael Fletcher. I was here yesterday and I came again to use the Internet. Would this be possible?"

"Certainly, dear, just make yourself comfortable here at the desk next to me and place your ID on the little square scanner. Same procedure as usual. I will be with you in ten seconds."

Michael followed all the instructions once more and was already doing his first search a minute later. "So, let us find what there is or was between the judge and mayor," he said, speaking to himself, "I wonder, I wonder."

He typed the mayor's name as well as that of the judge's and received a number of hits. Randomly he clicked on them and scrolled down the various texts. Endless articles came up about the mayor and his successful career and all he had done for the town. Likewise, there were articles and images of the judge presiding in the court room. However, there was nothing really connecting the two. He continued to search with both surnames, several times, but only received independent features. Only one showed both of them at an annual summer festival to celebrate the town's traditional farming festival.

He decided again for another search on the mayor and landed at an article about the city's prison and its integration of prisoners into society once released. It was followed by a report on the financing and the advantage for the city of the low costs of running the prison. With one hundred detainees and the standard cost of running a prison far below its budget, the town had an amazingly comfortable cashflow. Allocated national funds for the prison were in excess and were able to be used for the benefit of the community. The mayor was praised in almost every paragraph about the wonderful service he had rendered as a civil servant. The praise was so extensive that the editor must have used a thesaurus to get all the positive adjectives on his traits into the article.

He clicked onto various links and arrived at a report describing the miracle of the mayor on financing. The financing and balance sheet of the prison was all public record and could be read in a further section. He still had two hours at his disposal before the library would shut down. So, he decided to have a peek at it, but not for too long; he was more intrigued by the connection between the judge and the mayor.

Michael was an economist and had also chosen business as a side subject. He knew how to read balance sheets, the accounts of profit and loss and the principles of funding. After so many years away in prison though, he struggled a bit with all the numbers. He wondered if it was at all possible to finance a prison with minimal interests and get all the money back through the taxes of companies building the place. He remembered what Tom had told him about the clever model which almost self-funded the prison.

All expenses were neatly displayed. The balance sheet was laid out with assets on one side and the liabilities on the other. What struck him though was that there were almost no loans or long-term liabilities. *Another day,* he thought to himself, *to look at this more closely, but not now.*

He closed the site and decided to start anew. He typed in *Judge Carter* and started reading once more different articles on his career and his background. The judge went to a renowned university and studied law. He clicked on the link and there was an old photo of his graduation which was added to an article. There he was, standing proudly in the first line, a lot younger, but still with the same expression as today. Michael then stopped and zoomed in. There was absolutely no mistake. Next to him stood Mayor Hayden. It was confirmed at the bottom when he saw both names, clearly portrayed: *Standing in the front row: John Hayden and Jason Carter.*

"I do not believe this!" Michael exclaimed. He looked around hoping that nobody heard him speaking too loudly. He looked back at the screen and now had another part of the puzzle. Judge Carter and the mayor knew each other, not just superficially, but attended university together and finished law the same year from a very renowned university. So, buddies at universities. He knew the bonds that were created. They also stood next to each other, which confirmed his suspicion further. He continued to look at the photo, leaning back and shaking his head.

He swallowed hard. For him it was unimaginable, that it was a friend's favor, that the judge actually passed such a high sentence . . . but it was seemingly true. There was so much information coming together. The mayor running for another consecutive term in office, his son killed, the judge presiding the trial, and Michael sent to the same prison, probably under the supervision of the mayor, and all the people connected to him disappearing. Now it was all coming together like a puzzle that he had started twenty-six years ago. Just a few more pieces were still missing. The word *puzzle*, the same word that Jack had used only some days ago. He needed to find them all, to complete the full picture, to reveal the full truth. What difference it would make to his life he did not know. Nobody could give him back that dear time that had been so brutally and unjustifiably stolen.

What was he to do now that he was so close to the truth? He typed into the search bar once more the name of John Hayden to get his name and face back on the screen. There he was, old and retired, but with a big smile, still posing for the public, seemingly. Even his address was indicated, and below a small article about an honor cocktail lunch to celebrate his achievements, with invited guests. Even the press will be there to attend the event, at 2 Crescent Close. Michael looked at him and felt disgust at the image of the mayor, laughing in his face. He decided to log off and leave.

On his way out, Michael waved at the security officers at the entrance and wished them a pleasant afternoon. He walked slowly down the steps onto the street. As he exited the library compound, he congratulated himself on his ability to have been able to find the missing link, all on his own. The link that connected the mayor and the judge. The excessive sentence that he had received was seemingly all orchestrated by the mayor, for the pure reason of hatred and maximum suffering, as revenge for the killing of his son. It was the only plausible explanation why the judge could have become so influenced. However, a judge, a trier of law? He wondered if there was a deeper, more profound reason. One thing he was now certain of, and it was something he had guessed a long time ago; it was a personal matter.

He was very disturbed by his finding and wondered what to do next. Was the judge really the father-in-law or was it just a strange coincidence that he saw a girl with identical eyes to those of Jack. It was a question that hung in the air. Michael had a two-hour walk ahead of him back to Jack's house to speak and to confront him. If his assumption was true, then why had Jack been so eager for Michael to meet him?

Michael walked aimlessly along the street, pondering and arranging in his head all the information he had collected. He was so absentminded that he carelessly crossed the road without looking left or right. All of a sudden, a car came to an abrupt halt just next to him. He was startled and was about to apologize to the driver as two elderly people got out of a taxi. Michael watched them as they closed the door. He was still a bit shocked, and then peered at the cab driver, maybe for a second too long. The driver tilted his head and leaned out.

"Hello sir, can I help? If you need a ride, I have just become free."

The least Michael had expected was to be asked for a taxi ride but still had to digest that he had blindly ran in front of a car, only realizing now that the driver had stopped in time thanks to the end of the ride of the elderly couple.

As abruptly as the car had stopped, Michael spontaneously answered, "Yes, thank you indeed."

As he made himself comfortable the driver asked, "Where to?"

"2 Crescent Close, please." Michael had no idea why those words came out of his mouth. He had no intention whatsoever of seeing the mayor; it was just an internal reflex. His mind was battling with something very deep within, shooting information from neuron to neuron.

"2 Crescent Close it is, you are the customer," the driver voiced.

As the taxi drove off, Michael realized how silly it was to enter the taxi, let alone be driven to this address. What could he possibly do when he got there? And, if he really had the chance to see or meet him, what was there to say? He was convicted as guilty and the mayor did not know otherwise. He still bore more than a grudge on him; he was, after all, the murderer of his son. A few days back, he had absolutely no intention of finding the mayor. It was something he had already discussed with Jack. Michael was on the verge of asking to turn around when the driver interrupted his thoughts.

"Well, sir, I do not know if you had intended to come to his reception today. The event has already finished. Lots of people I can say. The couple that I had just let out, I collected them from that place. They were maybe the last ones to have left the mayor's party, which is at least what they told me. Many folks came today to this gathering–my boss was a happy man I can tell you. Everyone had to take a cab. Apparently, the host did not spare the alcohol. Journalists were also present, I was told. A popular guy this one, everyone speaks very highly of him."

"Can't say I agree with them." Michael was surprised at his own comment.

The driver looked quickly at Michael and grinned. "Well, seems you must have different political opinions then. Let me guess, you intentionally missed his party and go there now to mock him, eh?"

"Full house, sir. You cannot have put it any better."

The driver chuckled and drove on.

Twenty minutes later they had arrived in front of a large mansion. It was close to the neighborhood of Judge Carter, on the eastern fringe of town. Michael paid and tipped the driver, then thanked him. As he got out, he looked around to get a better impression of the place. The street was so clean you could have had dinner on it. Right in front of him a huge Victorian style mansion stood glamorously beyond a graveled passageway.

CHAPTER 21

The Mayor

The estate was fully enclosed by high black wrought iron bars. The lawn was well trimmed and endless flowerbeds were planted in the terrain to the sides of the path leading up. The thick iron gates stood wide open, so he decided, without further ado, to take a step towards the estate.

Michael guessed that the gates were still open to allow the catering services or the last journalists to leave. His assumption was confirmed as a van came down along the road. He stepped aside to let it pass. On the side, in bold red letters, was written *Finest Delicacies*. He continued to walk up the path glancing at the mansion, with its large multiple windows. He arrived at a small flight of steps. He walked up and entered through an open wood-paneled double door and found himself in a large entry hall with a high ceiling. The place was expensively furnished with a large chandelier hanging from above. Melodies of classical could be heard from a passageway to the right. On the left a winding flight of marble steps led to the next floor. High vases of flowers were placed in every corner. Waiters were buzzing around with full trays of empty dishes. There was still an aroma of oysters and champagne in the air. Michael just stood there and watched, admiring the tasteful furniture displayed and the thick dark red carpet. The sound of a vacuum cleaner could be heard in the distance.

He reckoned that the chance of seeing the mayor might be pretty high. After all, where else would he be? He was the host and his guests had only just left. As Michael strained his neck to look in all directions, he was struggling with what his conversation opener would be if he really did manage to see the mayor. However, he didn't have much time to consider the question, as an elderly man, dressed in an expensive dark cashmere suit, starched white shirt and a matching tie cleared his throat just behind him. His black shoes were so shiny the chandelier reflected in the leather.

"Excuse me, gentleman, may I be of any help?" He was tall, wore thin-framed gold glasses and had a nice tan. His hair was thick and grey, perfectly combed back. Michael at once recognized him. It was the mayor. He looked older than he appeared in the photos.

"I do not remember seeing you at the reception today. May I ask you your intent?" He eyed Michael curiously, inspecting him from top to bottom. Michael was clearly out of place.

"Sir, my name is," with hesitation and careful thought he completed his sentence, "it is *Brian* Fletcher."

"Well Mr. Fletcher, to what do I owe the honor?" he said in a tone that was very polite, but with a sense of boredom. "I have had a rather tiresome afternoon. I do believe you are not invited here and are neither part of the staff."

"You may not know me, but you may … know or remember my brother … his name is Michael Fletcher."

As Michael worded the full name, he saw that the color on the old man's face drain from tanned to white. He started staggering and had difficulties staying upright, so great was the shock he had received.

"Young man, just grab my elbow, please, and guide me to the guest area here to the right."

Michael stepped closer and helped him with a bit of reluctance. He hooked himself under his shoulder and supported a wobbling mayor the few steps to sit down on a white felt sofa in an adjacent reception hall. Several chairs and tables were spread out and a huge fireplace emitted warmth with the last logs burning down in a grate. The sofa had two little low glass tables on either side. On one of the tables was a tall empty latte macchiato glass with a long spoon stuck inside. At that moment Michael remembered Jack's words from this morning when he had been dropped off to see the judge. *I hope you got your long spoon with you.* Now he understood the meaning; *long enough to have a dessert with the devil.* He looked at the mayor and regarded him as if he were Satan himself. Michael took a chair and placed himself slowly in front of the sofa, facing the old man.

The mayor was about the same age as the judge but could have been taken for a considerable number of years more. He looked like someone who had been struggling all of his life to achieve something special and was worn with the effort. Whether it was the latter or whether it was really the broken heart caused by his son's death, it did not matter to Michael. He was here for another purpose.

"Thank you for helping me here. I have a bit of an issue with my low blood pressure, well, let us say, your visit has caused it to drop even further. Hearing that man's name was the last thing I had expected."

Michael watched him intensely as his face retook some of his color. He took out a white handkerchief from his inside pocket and dabbed his face, still breathing heavily. "I do say, neither did I expect any family member to appear here, especially without having been invited." He took a few more breaths and looked at Michael, regaining his composure. A suspicious glint had appeared in his eyes and after so much politeness he suddenly snapped, "What do you want?"

Michael was baffled by the sudden attack and change of composure. He remembered he had not had a chance to prepare his conversation opener after all, but then his intuition quickly brought him back on track. He was playing the fictitious brother.

"I wanted to tell you that my brother is not well. The years in prison have taken their toll. I came to see you to tell you this."

Defiantly the mayor replied, "He was rightly punished for this serious crime; I will never be able to condone. He deserved what he got. And now you are here reminding me unnecessarily by appearing. Why on earth have you dared to come here?"

But instead of answering, Michael now was on the roll. He had a concept he wanted to follow, all geared up. He had a frail man in front of him and wanted to seize the moment. "It was a rather harsh ruling, wasn't it?"

"He was condemned for what he did." The mayor almost shook as he said this.

"Was he really rightfully judged?" Michael intervened, quickly.

"He was sentenced in court."

Michael felt that the mayor was too wise and clever, like any politician. Especially one with a long career behind him, he would not step falsely too easily. So, he decided to pose a direct question. "Do you believe he really merited twenty-six years?"

"He received what he deserved," the mayor responded cold-heartedly.

Michael did not want to come to the direct accusation first. He still had two aces up his sleeve. The further the conversation went the more favorable it may become for him. He wanted to get the mayor wrong-footed and hoped to keep the conversation going. "Was the sentence given in direct relation to the alleged crime?"

A sign of unease crossed his face as the question was posed. The answer of the mayor came hesitantly. He obviously wanted to avoid the question and steer in a different direction. Again, as a good politician he perked up his face and met his gaze. "It was the judge's decision after all, young man," he said, decisively. "But I really do not understand why we are having this … let us call it a brief exchange? You should not be here; I recommend that you leave. I could have you arrested for trespassing."

Michael understood quickly that the mayor was not willing to entertain him for much longer. But decided to hold on to his first ace.

"The judge's decision … it really was his alone? Or, let me word it in a different way. Did you and Judge Carter have a certain understanding of the severity of the sentence?"

The mayor's mouth sagged open instead of denying the direct accusation made. It was a sign that Michael had hit home. A notion of agitation crossed his face. Was the mayor an old politician who had lost his sharpness? In younger years he would not have even flinched.

"What are you talking about, Mr. Fletcher?"

Michael decided to pull his first ace. "You did know each other rather well, you and the judge, I suppose?"

"What are you implying? This conversation is over. Please leave, now!"

Michael remained calm and eyed his opponent carefully, as if he were playing cards. He did not want to throw his last ace now, even though Michael knew he would not have much time before he really needed to get up and leave. He wanted to certainly avoid a heated exchange at the doorstep. He needed to gain time, to make the mayor reflect.

"You knew each other well since your university time. The sentence was a personal favor, nothing else. Twenty-six years was not appropriate, but your friend the Honorable Judge Carter fulfilled your wish to give Michael a long suffering, didn't he?"

The mayor was fully aware of the predicament he was in and did not want to give an impression of weakness. Neither did he have the energy to simply get up and leave, let alone take Michael by the arm to make him exit. He was still feeling too weak. Now he played for time by flicking a piece of dust from his dark trouser leg. He was seemingly no longer in such a hurry for his uninvited guest to leave.

"Someone sent you?" he finally voiced in a calmer and certainly more diplomatic tone.

"No, sir. I came on my own volition. As I said, my brother has been released and he wants to have answers that he had never received. Twenty-six years was an exceedingly long suffering, why so long?"

The mayor just thought for a moment and tried to compose himself, still trying to gain time. He was about to say something when he held back. Michael decided to wait. He wanted the answer from his mouth and looked expectantly at his host.

Finally, the mayor's composure sank as if crumbling together. Looking into the distance, he said, "Whatever the length," he swallowed hard and then continued, "it will not bring my son back, ever. Even today, after such a long time, the sense of loss is unfathomable."

It was no longer a political answer, but a response to suffering. That Michael was certain of. He wondered how much he should dwell upon the subject. He was though now sure; his man had exerted a significant influence on his sentence. Yet he wanted to let one last statement float the room.

"My brother spoke to me only a few weeks before his release. He swore it was not him."

The mayor came back to reality after having wandered off after his last statement. "One should stand for the crime one has committed."

Michael drew his last ace, one he wanted to sit and one he wished the mayor to remember. "He asked me to pass you the message that he is sorry for the crime committed–nobody wishes the death of a son–but in this case the wrong person was sentenced. Justice was not served. The real murderer of your only son is still out there, roaming around, and not punished."

A flicker of unease crossed the mayor's face.

"I hope you can live with that guilty conscience of having inflicted severe harm on an innocent person." Michael wanted to drive the dagger deeper. It would be his only consolation for revenge. "Whatever your achievements in life, you could not avenge the killer of your son. If hatred gets in the way, then the truth is hindered."

Michael looked deep into the mayor's eyes to come across as credible as possible. After all, it was his only purpose now that he had uncovered the truth.

The mayor sat there, shoulders slumped, hollow-eyed and frail. Even his fine tan could not hide the pain that dispersed in his face; it was probably the first realization in his life that he had once been wrong. After a long stare and another deep breath, the mayor finally voiced, weakly, "Then I am sorry, deeply sorry. But this will not change anything. Nothing can be changed anymore. Unfortunately, nobody can turn back the clock to remediate anything done and change what has already occurred in life."

Michael did not want to remain any longer. It was all said. He slowly got up and looked one last time at a crushed old man, his heart beating strongly. He left the big house without a further word, as surreptitiously as he had entered, hearing a cell phone ring behind him.

The doors were still open and he stepped outside, down the steps and down the gravel path. Another van drove up, to which he gave way once more. He left the estate, looked left, then right, and at the sky to orient himself again, then headed west at a leisurely pace.

During the long walk Michael tried to assemble the events of the afternoon and also those of the past days. Tom and Vincent had been torn out of his life by force. The judge and the mayor were old companions making a deal on his sentence. The puzzle was taking shape and more pieces were added, making it bigger by the day. Two mysteries still lay uncovered. If the judge was really his father-in-law, why had Jack been so adamant for Michael to see him? The biggest mystery of all, of course, is the identity of the real killer. Perhaps he had to dismantle and reassemble some of the puzzle pieces again to get the correct picture.

Michael was exhausted when he reached the neighborhood of his destination. It was a long walk. It was not only a physical, but also mental tiredness. He had been spooned with so many events that he had difficulties arranging them all. He felt drained and depleted. The world had changed and he needed to adapt–that was one part of the revolving coin. But the other part was the diverse discoveries he had made concerning him personally. He was simply sickened by them, how all of these had deprived him of half of his life. He needed to liberate himself from the burden, to become mentally free again. That would be the only way out. To do this, he would have to have a final discussion with Jack today to collect a few more puzzle pieces. He wondered if he would be able to complete the picture, or if he still had to hunt for more.

CHAPTER 22

Jack

A cold wind was blowing beneath a darkening sky as Michael finally arrived. There was a light showing through the blinds as he approached the house. Jack was in. Two weeks had passed since he entered this place for the first time. He could not explain it, but he had the dim feeling this could be his last.

He turned the door handle and pushed the door. It was unlocked.

"Jack, hi, I am back."

There was no sound to be heard, so he walked straight through the main entrance, popping his head round the door before entering the living room. Jack sat there at the table, expressionless, staring vacantly at the wall. Something was amiss. No greetings, no movement. He just rested as if embalmed, with one hand on his lap and another holding a cup of coffee on the table. It was still full and had been standing there for some time; a strange texture had formed on the surface. Next to it was a set of black leather gloves, and on top of it, to the horror of Michael, a black revolver in a dark holster.

Michael felt uncertain as he took off his coat and laid it on the sofa. He walked across the room and then placed himself on a seat in front of him, on the other side of the table, peeking again at the revolver. Jack raised his head and looked at Michael, awoken from his trance. He did not react the way he always did, the joyful and self-confident character. Quite the contrary. He was timid, quiet, pensive and completely introverted.

"How was your day, Michael?" he asked, without a seeming hint of interest.

"Anything wrong Jack?"

Jack breathed in deeply. "Life can be complicated, really, it is not what it seems. Nice on the outside, like many presents, with a shiny wrapping and a huge bow. All nicely presented, but when you open up and look inside, it is different than what it appears to be."

Michael remained silent and contemplated his friend. He sat there dazed and unrecognizable; he was not his usual self. "Do tell me, Jack, what's up? Not curious about my visit today?"

"I got a call from him, my father-in-law himself." Jack sat there emotionless as he started to recount to Michael what happened. "He had told me to stay away from *his* family. He actually had the guts and cheek to call my wife and my daughter his family, can you imagine this? 'Never come again, never dare to see your daughter again,' he said."

Michael sighed, moving forward, but then sat back again. He was not going to lose his patience. He had all time in the world. It was time that Jack spoke. He would listen, even though the question was burning inside him. *What the hell happened?* Michael thought about his day, his discussion with the judge, his exchange with the judge's daughter and then he had seen that girl. Was the assumption he'd had the right one? Was it really Jack's daughter or was Jack on a completely different subject? He decided to wait and listen, patiently.

"He called me in the afternoon and simply said never to come again. Neither would I be allowed to meet my daughter next weekend. He was in a rage and threatened me if I didn't abide." Jack finally took his coffee and took a sip, pursing his lips and turning the corner of his mouth. The coffee was obviously cold. He put the cup down and continued. "You probably have no idea why, I assume. You do not know what he holds against me, and why. But I know what I hold against him. The question is simply, who has the stronger evidence and whose accusation bears more weight." Jack nodded slowly and then stared vacantly at the wall.

Michael was not sure at all what he meant. What accusations did they hold against each other? Instead of asking, he decided to simply continue to listen. But instead of receiving a sequel, Jack decided to stop and lightened up a bit out of the blue.

"So now you know why I am so devastated. Family issues, personal things, nothing to do with you. I need to solve them somehow. I am not going to let him get away with it." Jack stood up as if nothing had happened, asking while taking his cup, "Want a coffee, Michael? Then let us talk and you can tell me what happened today. Mine here has gone cold. I am making myself a new one."

It came really as a great surprise to him that Jack suddenly wanted to change the subject. Was his visit today after all not connected? Michael sat there and contemplated what to do. *Now or never, let us see if you were just playing Hyde a minute ago.* Without further ado, he decided to simply shout across the room, "Jack, I saw your daughter today." It was an audacious move. Maybe he was wrong. Maybe it was not his daughter, but he had had enough of the secrets.

Michael awaited some immediate reaction, but a moment of complete silence hung in the air. Instead of hearing the hot water kettle boil, there was absolutely no sound at all, and then a plonk of a cup being placed on the kitchen table. Seconds passed without any further commotion.

"All okay in there, Jack?" Michael twisted his head and glanced to where he had disappeared.

Slowly Jack came out of the kitchen, stepping like a warrior who had just lost a battle, and retook his seat again without his coffee. He looked at Michael emotionlessly and with a hint of surprise, tilting his head. "Well, I did not expect this. You really found out. A very astute observation, indeed."

They eyed each other wordlessly, both equally unsure what to say next. He was right. His discovery was true.

"I imagine your daughter is there every day, and it's likely you go to see her often."

Jack remained silent with his gaze fixed on Michael.

"Probably there is this rule that you are not even allowed to see her apart from the set time you were given. But you disregard it and observe from a distance. That is why you walk every day, when you told me in prison often that you are more of a walker."

Michael tilted his head, hoping Jack would respond, but Jack sat unmoving.

"Consequently, it's apparent that you saw the Judge on each occasion, and you were aware that he also frequented the location every afternoon to observe his granddaughter."

Jack regarded Michael sadly, almost with watery eyes and swallowed. "Yes Michael, he is a creature of habit; I knew he would be there. You are right." Jack sighed. "I went there every single day. I am only supposed to see her every two weeks. This is the somber agreement made, so I go and watch her from across the field, sadly. I wish I could have more of her. You cannot believe how hard this is for me."

"And every time he is also there, sitting on a bench."

Jack nodded solemnly. "Yes," he said in a quiet voice, barely audible. The garrulous personality had gone. The once talkative character, the positive thinker, had succumbed.

"The judge was greatly upset again when I spoke to him. I guess that is why he probably called you."

"Could be, maybe you were the trigger."

Michael studied Jack intensely and wondered once again why then Jack was so eager for him to see the judge, but then said, "I also spoke to your wife, just before I saw your daughter."

Jack looked up, with a sense of surprise. "How did you find out?"

"Coincidence I say, she has your eyes. However, the resemblance could not have been a coincidence." Looking across the room, Michael now understood why there were no photos of his family. Jack did not want him to recognize neither wife nor daughter when he was going to be sent to the park. Jack had had a strategy, right from the time Michael had entered this house.

Jack nodded, looking up at Michael. "Impressive Michael, I am indeed impressed."

"Explain to me Jack, now that we are on the subject, why did you divorce in the first place? What went wrong?"

Jack leaned back and let out a sigh. "It all started with the fact that I was often absent, an absent husband, when I began to work in the prison. We had our rows and fallings-out and then I always somehow made up for it again. Working nights, sleeping days, you do not really share a common interest. When she wanted to go out for dinner, I got prepared for work. When we watched TV, I fell asleep. We had a different biorhythm. It all still somehow worked out, until our daughter was born. We thought we would not have children, but God decided otherwise. Christine is eight years younger than me. She was already relatively old for children, but the doctors gave her the thumbs up since all the analyses always turned out positive. Daddy of course provided the most expensive medical aid you can imagine. It all went smoothly, without complications."

Michael sat there, listening intently, as Jack unfolded his life. He had known Jack for half of his own existence, but this part of the story had never been told. It had always been avoided. He decided not to interrupt, but just listen.

"So, all seemed to work out, after all. We named her Jackelyn; it was an addition to my name. I was so proud and elated when my wife agreed to this. The day she was born, I was the happiest person on earth. I was a dad. My worries, deepest sorrows and inner griefs had disappeared, as if they had lifted off in soap bubble and flew away, popping in another unknown place." Jack blinked and a tear ran down his cheek.

Michael watched him emotionlessly. "Please continue."

Jack breathed heavily and paused as if wanting to phrase something complicated. "You know what Jackelyn means? You probably don't." He did not look at Michael but continued to stare blankly at the wall ahead. "The name is Hebrew, and it originates from Jacob, son of Isaac as portrayed in the Book of Genesis, in the first testament of the Holy Bible. Jacob means 'May God protect.' I wanted God to protect her … but unfortunately, the name also has another very significant meaning … Jacob, he who held the heel of his twin brother Esau at birth, to ensure he was the first born. It therefore also means 'supplanter.' It basically means to take the place of and serve as a substitute."

Michael sat there wordless and felt a sense of pity as Jack breathed deeply. He then continued after a while, blinking. "That is what then happened. My daughter substituted me, and my wife lost complete interest in me. She spent entire days with her parents, even nights, entire weekends, taking our daughter with her. She was never there. So, as time passed, we fell apart. It was really my father-in-law, the judge who made life easy for her, rolling out the red carpet in his house. He pushed her to stay away from me. He was the one who was finally to blame for pulling us apart."

Michael just stretched a bit and listened intensely as Jack unfolded the forlorn story of how he had fallen out with his wife, pushed by her father. "How is it possible that a father-in-law can cause such a difference between you and your wife. He literally drove a wedge into your marriage."

Jack flinched, as if in pain. "A wedge you can call it, but the final wedge that led to our divorce came only later. An unfortunate event. Something happened that should not have occurred."

A moment of silence filled the room. Jack sitting there, pitying himself. His gloves and his revolver were still lying there on the small table, as if part of the room furniture. He took the revolver carefully, inspected it at close range and then laid it back on the table next to his gloves.

"You know, I really worshipped Christine. When I met her my life changed. It was the best thing that had ever happened to me so far. She was so precious, I was uxorious. However, then she was stolen from me." Jack paused as he gazed at the tabletop, but then resumed. "It is true. She had gone through a lot with my absenteeism, I agree, but we somehow always fixed it again … to simply continue. What that man did though, I simply cannot pardon and let him get away with it. You must understand—without my daughter I have nothing. He took my entire family."

Jack looked at Michael again, wanting to say something but not knowing where to start, finally clearing his throat. "Let me tell you a story. It happened a long time ago, Michael, before you even arrived in town. It is the start of everything, why it all … I do not know how to put it, turned out as it has … and when even eventually you became a part of it. You became part of everything that happened."

Michael looked at him, astonished, and wondered where he fitted into this narrative.

Jack sat back and folded his hands and looked down. "There was a young politician called John Hayden." Michael flinched at the name but kept quiet. *Now this is really becoming interesting,* he thought.

"The mayor has had a splendid career; I can tell you. He came along as the savior of the city. Elected and reelected. He did so much for this town. Popular, rich, and then pitied. Pitied, because his son was killed. It gave him further popularity. All he did, all his life, was to dedicate his political career to the people of this place, this town and city. If, however, you unveiled what was really behind all of this, Michael, it was nothing of the kind. There was no honesty. He was just vile, sleazy, and most of all corrupt." Jack looked back up as he continued. "And the prison was just the start of it. The whole corruption was camouflaged by building this bloody thing. All the accounts that were shown, all this self-funding of the prison, the low costs, it was just a swindle, a complete fraud. It was only there on paper to make the whole project look good. But it was never such a kind. The expenses were higher, the companies who built it cost more, the only thing that is really true is that the cost of running the prison was somehow lower. But it meant a much greater deal had to be spent than initially planned. You are an economist, check yourself and look at the numbers. They do not add up, that is what I was told by someone. Yes, someone special, who knew. So that is where it all began, Michael, where all the corruption started and what caused everything that had happened."

Michael had not told Jack about his discoveries at the library. His gut feeling of irregularities had been correct. Little loans, no long-term debts. How could it all be possible? Then the connection of the judge and the mayor, probably best buddies. "Did you know the mayor and the judge finished university together?"

Jack managed to emit a smile of appreciation. "You did your homework again. Indeed, Carter and Hayden finished university and that led to a special bond between the two. The judge supported the mayor's election and the mayor in turn ran the commission for the judge to become elected. At the time there was no due diligence, no panel or committee to check for any irregularities. You can call it what you want, nepotism, corruption. I help you, you help me, I pay him, and he helps you. You cannot imagine how much cash was passed between their hands. Everyone was happy and everyone benefited. So, Hayden became mayor and Carter became judge and the mayor built the prison, in record time, no expenses spared. He had them all in his hands. It did not finish there. The principal warden, you know, they called him *The Law,* and the mayor were also best friends, like the judge. All three of them were together at school. The warden simply did not do university. He went to the police, like I did. He joined the academy and was then made principal warden when the prison opened. Now you know who, and why, he checked the letters. His friend, the mayor, just told him to do so. I honestly did not know though to what extent. You never told me in prison that you had never heard from your lawyer. It is not a subject we had touched." Michael listened intensely, without even blinking. "The warden was put there by the mayor himself. He was asked personally by him to keep an eye on you. So, I guess, what Tom told you, about someone on the inside, here is the answer. It was he who spied on you. But it was not me."

Michael nodded. It sounded plausible. "Jack, why didn't you tell me ..."

"Let me continue my dénouement, the full event, why all occurred as it has ... what I just told you ... is only the tip of the iceberg of everything. Everyone knows everyone here in this district. The judge, the mayor, they are all connected. Michael, that is how politics works in this place and the mayor was the driving force behind all of it. He checked the general opinion and sold it as his idea, as if it were new. He then played the game in such a way as to gain more support from everywhere he could. If opinion changed, he swung the other way. That is politics Michael, that's classic politics. As long as you are a strong character, and you are able to show the others who follow you are also benefiting, they will all row in the same direction. And I can tell you how hard they rowed to keep up with the pace set. Everyone including ..." but then Jack broke off.

Michael waited for Jack to continue his story, but noticed he was taking a mental break. There was still a fundamental question, something which was still amiss. "Jack, I do not know if you have the answer, but I need to understand better why the judge passed such a severe sentence. Was it simply on the command of Mayor Hayden?" He saw Jack nodding. "So basically, you are saying that Judge Carter simply abetted his friend's wish, for just loyalty or to also get a share in the corrupted business?"

"I am not one-hundred percent sure, Michael, but I doubt very much that Carter was corrupt. I do not believe so; it was just a personal favor. But I had my one source, the same source who told me about the irregularities, the same person who also rowed hard at the mayor's pace. Now listen, that is the problem of the whole story and where it all began to go wrong."

Jack sighed deeply and looked Michael into the eyes. "That is why I also took the position in prison and left the service of police. It was to repent, to atone myself for my wrongdoing. To redeem for what I had done."

Michael looked at him surprisingly and wondered what was now to come. He sat back and peered at him suspiciously, waiting for Jack to unfold the rest of his story.

CHAPTER 23

Cat Out of the Bag

Jack wiped his mouth with the back of his hands along with the tears running down his cheek. Michael looked at him, patiently.

"Everything I just told you, I found out from a particular person, my source." Jack paused and then worded carefully. "Flynn Meier."

Michael smirked ironically, shaking his head slowly. "I should have realized, hell, you are the same age as Flynn; the cross, the same year of birth. You knew him and the scene at the graveyard. It was just played?"

"No Michael, it wasn't, I had never visited his grave. I knew it was here in town, but I swear, I never went to see him. I–I couldn't."

"Why not, if you knew him so well?"

"I did not have the courage; I did not go to his burial. I was simply not able to. Too well I knew him, too well, I just couldn't take it. It was a big step for me when we went there, hence therefore also my hesitation when you suggested it."

"I think you owe me some elaboration." But as Michael said this to Jack, there was no response. He just sat there with his glazed eyes peering somewhere into the distance. Michael waited, but he did not react. "What do you think, Jack? That you don't owe me a better explanation?" Michael voiced more loudly.

"Sorry, what did you say?" Jack dragged his thoughts back. "I am sorry, I drifted away."

"I asked you if you knew him so well, why didn't you go to his funeral?"

Jack breathed in and nodded. "Let me therefore give you the remainder of the story." Jack swallowed hard, wiping away more tears. "Flynn was like a brother to me; we grew up together. He arrived after his adoption and sat down in school next to me. It was like love at first sight. We were best friends, had the same interests, played the same sports, went to the same summer camps, chased the girls together. He was part of me and I was part of him. We were inseparable, even when we were already grown up. We shared all the joys and also the secrets. He became the owner of the casino by means of his father's influence. I joined the police academy. We regularly spent long nights after closure at the casino. All was new. Free drinks for me, the occasional shuffle of cards, for fun. All was so well. Well, it seemed to be, until one particular day, the same year after he took ownership. It was the early hours of one particular morning; he was extremely drunk and talkative and boasted about something I should never have been told. I remember his slurry words. He drank too much, there was so much temptation, so he just sat down somewhere, and some beautiful waiter just came and gave him his favorite cocktail. He also had to entertain his guests with a personal presence. So, he got used to the alcohol. By the time the casino closed we were the only two left, he was well beyond the limit that I would ever be. I took it more moderately due to my job. Well, it was not until that morning that he sat down with another drink in his hand and looked at me. He had this glare in his eyes and was pondering, licking his lips. I knew him well and waited. Finally, after another gulp he voiced, 'Do you know how much cash I have stashed away?' He smirked and took another sip at his beer. 'I lost count. There is so much, I do not care anymore. You know why? Every time I empty the box, and take it away, it is refilled again.' He grinned at me and said, 'I will show you tomorrow.'"

Michael leaned forward, listened intensely and nodded as Jack continued his story.

"Michael, I was not sure what he meant and let it pass. I assumed he had forgotten anyway, the conversation we had, when the following night he took me aside. He sat me down at a roulette table and whispered in my ear, 'Now watch, carefully.' He took over the table, thanked the croupier and told him to go home. He would finish the night. He took his position, fitting his white gloves on confidently. Quite a few players were left. They'd all had a lot to drink. The girls with short skirts served them so quickly they did not have the chance to finish their glass before the next one arrived, free of charge. Of course, just with one purpose. The more they drank, the more they risked and played, and of course the more they lost. I marveled at how much money was spent. You know that nobody wins in a casino. Nobody, not on a long-term basis, at least. A small stack was provided for me, so I could join the fun, when I suddenly got this ominous feeling that something was going to happen. Flynn had this grin on his face I recognized. He was up to something. But I could not have imagined what I would see next. Flynn smiled at me as another big pile of chips were raked away by him. Instead of putting them all neatly aside where they belong, he took three chips from the stack the bank won and pushed it into a secret hole in the table. He repeated the move regularly. Nobody saw it except me, because every time he did it, he hinted to me to look. I had lost count how often he repeated this during the night."

"So, you just sat there and watched?"

"What was I supposed to do? I placed the occasional chip to show I am staying engaged. But … Michael, you cannot believe how easy it was to create black money in that place. For every twenty or sometimes thirty chips the casino earned, one or more went into that mysterious hole. The casino declared a five to ten percent higher earning of the clients to compensate for the missing chips. The chips were changed by Flynn the same evening for cash, which he stashed away underground! What I just told you he even said to me personally. The guests had long gone, and Flynn was his usual self, confident. 'I hope you have a watchful eye. You noticed what I did with one or the other chip that the bank won. Easy money, already exchanged for cash. We just declare the extra win to the customer. I can make as much as I desire.' Michael, you cannot believe how shocked I was. I had not expected this. Me, a force of the law, and here my best friend admitting to fraud, a serious crime. I asked him how long this had been going on. He said, smiling to me, that it all started just before the building of the prison."

Jack sat there and shook his head, looking Michael in the eyes, as if asking for help. "Michael, I wanted to leave and just get out. I felt disgust. Somebody I had known for such a long time, whom I trusted with my life, now admitted to such unthinkable means to hoard money. I was shocked, I asked him what all this cash was for, and he said to me again in a usual slurry drunken voice, 'If I tell you, you must join the business. My father will reward you well. After all, a good copper is useful when I have to deliver the money. I was asked to get personal protection on board, so I thought of you. I can trust you, can't I?' I was bewildered and then I asked again what his father had to do with it, after which he then opened up. 'You know well that it is necessary to pay hands here and there to make this prison operation a success. Once a week, I take it all and bring it to my father. He deals the money, as if it were cards. So many hands are at the table, you won't believe it. It is money, which satisfies everyone to do as he says. You do not believe that this whole prison operation can be run without it, do you? This self-funding event is a scam.' His voice had been so slurry at times I had difficulties understanding what he said. His father, the mayor, instigated all of this to keep his reputation, his promise, his low budget and just used the money to keep everyone quiet. They were all involved. The construction companies, his staff, even the auditors, who filed false statements. As long as the money came flying in, everyone was happy and looked the other way, as there was simply no shortage. A lot of the cash was stashed away by the mayor himself, used for other bribes and luxurious life. He was a politician and had to fund his campaigns and most of all he had to keep people happy. And his son, Flynn, was certainly just as content to play along–his life was secured."

"Did Flynn try to pay you off as well, Jack?"

"Of course. 'How much do you want?' he said to me numerous times. Michael, I swear, he tried, but I refused. I joined the police to enforce the law. He underestimated me. I wanted him to stop and told him that it would not be too late. We could go public; declare the fraud and he would get off probably without harm as he came forward. But he just laughed. 'You cannot be serious,' he said to me. 'This is too easy money. Do you really think anybody will believe you? There is no evidence.' He looked at me sternly and said, 'Next Friday, be there, early hours of the morning. At closure, I have a big sum of money to deliver. Be there by midnight. I need someone to be with me. Ensure you do not come in uniform, too visible. Remember, next Friday.'"

Michael shook his head in disbelief and wanted to say something, but then decided otherwise.

"You cannot believe the week I passed. I just could not concentrate on my job. I was out there patrolling and drove regularly by the prison, which had been already completed a few months back. New inmates arrived by the day, transferred from other places. And every time I saw that place, I thought about Flynn, my friend, and his confession to me. The days passed by and of course Friday approached. He even left a message on my answering machine. 'See you tonight, old pal, I want to invite you for a drink.' That is all there was, but I knew better, so I decided not to go. I wanted no part of this. Unfortunately, I changed my mind. It was the mistake of my life. I left, just a bit too late." Jack stopped and shut his eyes tightly as more tears ran down his face.

Michael leaned further forward, eyeing Jack carefully. He almost guessed what was to come. Jack breathed deeply and the color drained from his face as the tears ran down.

"I left my car somewhere far away. I did not want to be seen and walked to the casino. I was not far away when I saw a familiar gait. I knew it was Flynn and stopped at exactly the same place where we had stood the other night. I wanted to confront him and ask him to turn back. But all he did when he saw me was say, 'At last, I thought you'd never come. Where is your car? I had to leave mine. Imagine I got caught this particular night drunk and driving.' He actually laughed at his own joke. I told him to stop, not to do this. It was not too late. Now I had seen him; I had become a witness. However, what he had told me was not in the records. I told him to simply stop, to go back to the casino and leave the money. He started shouting at me to mind my own business and to get out of my way. He went crazy. I tried to reason with him, but to no avail. I could smell his alcohol level. It must have been high as usual. And then he just wanted to push me and step past. I held him on his shoulder. We pushed and shoved; he just did not want to go back. 'Just mind your own bloody business,' he shouted. I remember those words so well. I was not angry at him, just shocked. Then I grabbed him by both shoulders and screamed, 'Listen to me, please, come to your senses, please!' I basically begged. I just did not know what to do. I tried to tell him in a calm manner that he was doing something illegal, that it was not in his very nature to do."

Jack blinked, looked at the ceiling and breathed in heavily, drying his face with his sleeve. He squinted his eyes, which were burning from the flow of tears. Then he looked directly at Michael, his eyes red and puffy. Michael returned the gaze calmly. Then he noticed his friend's facial expression started to change completely, as if a shadow of a ghost had appeared. He became completely white.

"Michael … he suddenly pulled a knife. I really do not know where it came from. It was somewhere, probably in his inner pocket or in the back of his trousers. It was one of these switchblades. You know, where you press the button and the blade flips open. I did not even know he had one. He held it up and threatened me. 'Hell, what are you doing?' I shouted at him. I was so perplexed and surprised, you cannot imagine. Your best friend, my brother in heart, pulling a knife at me, menacingly. It was so unexpected that I completely forgot who was in front of me. I saw this shiny thing before me, and I felt my life was under threat. Imagine: it's dark and you see this huge weapon being pointed at you. Do you have any idea what a tremendous shock this was for me? I–I wanted to step back, but my police instinct told me something else. I was trained to do something different. In the police force we learn about aggression and being attacked with weapons. We spent hours, years, with martial art experts, flying on the mat, training with eyes blind-folded until the gesture and movement was perfected. You must react in a split-second, otherwise your life can get wiped out. There is no time to think when you are attacked. It is like catching a ball when someone throws it at you. What do you do when someone pitches a ball at your face?"

"I throw up my hands and catch it, or at least try to deflect," Michael said calmly.

"Exactly, it is instinct that does it for you. When you throw a ball at a small kid, he blinks, and it hits him. He must learn instinct. The same way we in the police had learned to react without thinking when you get attacked. Point a gun at my head, at close range. I swear I can take it off you before you even manage to pull the trigger. So good we had become, so well we were instructed. I had him with both of my hands on his shoulders when I saw this knife coming towards me. I acted as if it was the most natural thing. I let go and stepped back a bit. He continued to push it towards me with his right hand. Maybe not to attack me, but just to keep his distance. Michael, I have replayed this scenario every day for the last twenty-six years. I have no explanation. The blade came forward, I moved to the right and with my left hand I thrust his hand upwards, grabbing his wrist, maybe too hard, but there was absolutely no resistance. He probably did not expect my reaction. He was drunk after all. So fast was my movement that I turned the knife 180 degrees, and this idiot fell forward into the blade. At first, Michael, I did not realize. He just stood there, looking down at me with the knife in my hand, having it thrust right into his stomach. My world completely crumbled. It was like my wildest nightmare ... but I was awake. It felt like a ton of stones crushing onto my shoulder. My friend, my best friend, I had just, well, I–I really did not know what I had just done. Hurt him, seriously hurt, or even killed him. I just do not know what I felt in that fraction of a second. Michael, believe me, I had no intention! My whole vision became blurred, the street swam before me, the shimmering of low lights around me became soft and then he crumbled, right in front of me onto the ground, while I just stood there. I was under tremendous shock, hardly able to breathe. And then–then I heard these steps approaching behind me. Someone was coming."

"Me."

"Yes, Michael, you. It was you. That I learned later. Why the hell did you have to arrive that very moment?"

"I have been asking myself that very same question thousands of times."

"I panicked, Michael, nothing else. I wanted to first mingle in the dark as you arrived, but thought it to be too risky, so I ran. I just wasn't myself and decided to just dart away. I sprinted up the small street. I don't even recall passing Eileen on the way. I simply do not remember. All I did was to go as fast as I could, running as quickly and as long as my feet could take me. I did not stop until I was home. I left the car where it was. The rest of the story you know."

When Jack had confessed his sin, he put his hands on his thighs, looked down and leant forward with his eyes completely transfixing the ground. Michael sat there emotionless and just watched him. He was not sure what to think, let alone say.

CHAPTER 24

Contrition

They sat there for what seemed like minutes. Michael replayed his life; the day he had come to this town, the evening he spent with his friends and then the indictment, his life in prison and finally his last few days with Jack. These two weeks had been one of his happiest times, the happiest he could remember. He was with someone who cared, helped, and comforted him. He had someone he could trust, a living soul that listened, someone to share the pain and someone who had answers. But as quickly as it all began, it ended. He had been deceived. Who actually cared about him now? Nobody was left. Even his parents had deserted him. As Michael remembered his mother, he recalled again his encounters with Eileen.

Michael leant forward. "So, Jack, now we know at least it was you who Eileen had seen running past her, and I understand also now why you dropped me off at her place and disappeared. But after a fleeting encounter twenty-six years ago, you don't even recall? How could she possibly recognize you?"

Jack looked up at him neutrally. "I darted past her in the obscure passageway, but I did not even remember her. It was only until I read the transcript of the court hearing that I found out about a witness that saw me." Mockingly he smirked and grunted, "You never know about women. You'd be surprised at what they are capable of. They have incomprehensible memories, for certain things, of course. They tend to remember the strangest things, not just birthdays. A small flashback and she would probably recognize me."

Michael felt bitterness. He had been used as a stand-in for something he had not committed. Sporadic events popped up in his head and the injustice that he had to suffer. "So, all this pushing for me to visit the judge ... what I am not sure I understand is why you insisted so much that I speak to him? Just a well-planned decoy?"

"No, it wasn't, it had a purpose."

"Your purpose, but no other. Did he know it was you?"

"No, my father in-law had no idea. My wife did not know. Nobody knew it was me. Nobody ever found out. I was the only person with the secret. It was only during the last few years, as I struggled to accept that my wife did not want to come back to me, pushed certainly by her father, that I confronted him. It was probably the most stupid thing I did, but I was in a rage. I went to him one evening and accused him, full of exasperation, of having been influenced by the mayor, his best friend and political ally. He was indeed an exceptionally good friend of the mayor; they met often and supported each other in their professional life, wherever possible. It was certain that he acted on behalf of the mayor's wish to indict you. I said to him that he misused his position in court, just as favor, when he passed your sentence. I touched a raw nerve certainly. I wanted to hurt him, even threaten him. He was startled that I came up with such a thing so many years later. By his reaction, I knew my assumption was right. He is an intelligent guy though, highly intelligent, someone who reads people like nobody else, and he connected the dots. And then he let it spurt out, 'I never believed Michael Fletcher did it. There was just no motive,' he said to me. 'You knew Flynn, he was your best friend. But why did you kill him?' When he said that, I did not answer, but he had hit home. I just sat there. I did not have a response. I had asked myself the same question over the last few years. Probably I pondered too long on the significance of his question and the possible answer. Only at that moment did he know for certain. It was a shot in the dark by him, but he had really hit the target. I could have bluntly denied it, as there was no proof. But the accusation got to me badly, and I felt guilty. Never had anybody ever dreamt of accusing me, so I managed to hide my guilt and inner sorrow up to that point. I had not been stricken up in any inquest. I had not even been questioned. But this direct accusation, Michael, was simply too much for me, too much to take."

"That is therefore the real reason then why matters between you two went to this extent. He hated you for what you did, and he also despised you, because you accused him. You attacked him, so he retaliated. And he probably forced you to accept a divorce."

"Yes, it was then that matters became worse between us. As the years went by, he pushed my wife to file for divorce."

"So, you also developed a hatred, and I was your tool for revenge. You wanted me to push him to admit his wrongdoing during the trial. It was personal, nothing else, was it? You had planned this whole thing for years. All these investigations, the visits to Eileen, Tom, Vincent and then the repeated visit to your father-in-law. It was nothing but a hoax, a bad diversion, for personal revenge."

"If the marriage had survived, I would not have gone this far. Christine was never told the truth. She has no idea that I am a guilty soul. This way he had me in his hands, he promised me that if I accept the divorce, it would never be known to anyone. The only revenge I could have therefore possibly gotten was using you, yes."

Michael moved forward in his seat, stunned. It was a pitiful sight, as Jack was slumped in his chair, completely devastated. However, all he felt now was utter disgust. Jack was the culprit; he was the reason he'd sat innocently for twenty-six years locked away in prison. All the company given by him, the friendship, the advice and his care in the last days ... it was all wiped away in a blink of an eye.

"And you are still trying to get away with it, after you have now confessed?"

"Believe me, I was a prisoner myself for twenty-six years, peering behind that hole, a very lonely prisoner."

Michael looked at him blankly, shaking his head, feeling no pity, even though he knew Jack tried to make up for it as much as he could.

"The day I killed Flynn, my best friend, my life had ended. Then I followed your process and saw you sentenced. What more could I do now, but to atone myself for what I had done? It was the reason I left the police force and decided to join you in prison. Every night I came to work, every night we spoke, for twenty-six years. I was punished for the wrongdoing I had committed. I do not see it personally as a crime; I just killed him completely involuntarily. If I had given myself in, I would have probably even been found innocent, in the eyes of the law. But deep inside me, I knew I would never be free again. I would remain guilty for life. The day God gave me a daughter I had thought I was forgiven. But here I was gravely mistaken. My actual punishment only began when she was taken away from me soon after. The growing up of my daughter was the instrument to complete my final suffering. It was like a death sentence during my imprisonment these final years, as I saw my wife disappear with her."

"You pretended to be my friend, but you betrayed me, from the first moment we met. And all these last days here, just for show?"

"Betrayal you can call it, but *betrayal* has a much deeper significance. Jesus was betrayed by Judas; however, Jesus let it happen, because only through his crucifixion he was able to fulfil God's purpose. He redeemed humanity and cancelled our sins."

Michael did not understand what Jack was trying to imply and looked at him in disgust as Jack continued.

"Look Michael, I know what I caused, and I know that you went to prison for what I did. There are no words for this. All I can say is that I am deeply sorry for what happened to you. But believe me, I suffered just as much as you."

As Michael sat there, he did not know what to feel. He looked pitifully at him. Who, finally, was the prisoner and who sat twenty-six years in punishment? Well, Michael knew who had really lived out the time *behind* bars. It was difficult for him to imagine that it was really the other way round. Michael did not know whether to feel hate or mercy. The mix of these feelings was so strong that one overwhelmed the other. He *was* betrayed, but not just by Jack, by so many others as well. Who had committed the biggest of betrayals, he was not really sure. Jack, the judge, the mayor or even Tom to some extent. Vincent had also played his part by not trying hard enough. One thing was sure: nobody was innocent. Only Eileen. She had pity. Could he blame her for anything, or could she have persisted more during the trial? The more Michael thought, the more he found blame and fault in everyone. Last but not least, was he himself at fault? Had he not drunk so much that night, he may have never acted as he did, he may not have overturned the body and may have not left that fat fingerprint on the knife. But how can he blame himself? He was just at the wrong place at the wrong time. It was destiny that finally brought him there. Surely, he was not at fault.

After a while Jack looked up and took his gloves that were next to the revolver and put them on, slowly and meticulously. "You know what these gloves are?" He paused and checked them occasionally while fitting them tightly, looking at Michael. "This is the reason why there were no prints. I had worn exactly this pair when I confronted Flynn. The finest pair of leather gloves the police could have provided."

Michael watched Jack fasten the wrist strap tightly. Then he looked at the revolver, lying there in its holster, to the right of Jack and then back at him. He could not stand the sight of Jack anymore; it was time to leave and to never come back. He remembered what Tom had told him only a few days ago. His client's name was also Michael. He wanted to sell all and live as a Buddhist monk. Maybe it was a possibility, to leave and at least start anew. He had enough money. Michael got up slowly, looked across at Jack and went to the sofa for his coat without taking a final peek at his old friend. There was nothing to say. It was over.

"This revolver, Michael, was never given back. After my transfer to prison, I kept it. There is no record of it anymore. They must have forgotten about it," Jack said in a slow and loud tone. "It has been lying in my kitchen drawer for years."

Michael listened, disinterested, without turning around. He put on his coat and pulled it down tightly. As he did so he heard Jack pull the gun slowly out of its holster. First the click of the strap-button of the casing and then the brushing of the gun against its interior.

"Death seals everyone's lips, did you know this, Michael?" Jack shouted.

The noise of placing the holster onto the table was immediately followed by the hammer of the revolver cocking. It was a sound that startled Michael for a moment, but it did not impede his committed step towards the front door. He was about to reach the exit and touch the door handle when he heard the clicking of the cylinder of the gun. His posture stiffened slightly. However, he did not turn around. Instead, he was determined to leave the room, wordless, when he heard a muzzle blast right behind him, the gunshot echoing loudly. He stopped and waited for the pain to arrive. He was certain that Jack had shot him. He continued to stand there for a while, close to the door, ready to open it, with his back facing Jack. He touched his shoulder, but the pain did not manifest. Instead, he heard the thud of a body falling behind him.

He stood still for a short moment, pondering upon the situation but did not bother to look behind. Instead, Michael opened the door, waited on the doorstep, and peered out. It was like another déjà vu. A new step into freedom, the same step he took a few days ago, when he left prison. *What will await me now?* he asked himself.

He turned up the collar of his coat, slipped his hands into his pockets and stepped into the cold air. He left the door open and walked away. He had not managed to clear his name, as his innocence could probably never be proven now. But there was at least one consolation he could cling to for the rest of his life: he had discovered the truth. Much harm was done, not just to him, he had learned, but also to other people all over the world. Many innocent people suffered during his prison time. He decided, though, not to pity himself anymore, but to embrace the rest of his life. Not to look back, but forward. Tomorrow would be his birthday—he somehow remembered it now. He would light a small candle for himself and look at it in solitude, but with a glint of hope, that the light shining would give him courage for his next step into a completely new existence.

Reflection from the Author

I wonder every day if we take a moment to stop and review what we have done before moving onto the next task. In this fast-paced world, we often act without being able to reflect. An electronic message is answered in the blink of an eye. Do we really take our time to think about what we write or say? Or is this taken by the expectation of having to respond equally as fast?

Michael Fletcher's story mirrors the change of the world. We are moving so fast, and we all try to keep up. A great majority of the population today finds it more and more difficult to keep the pace.

If you took a harmonica and you placed it sideways on the floor and slowly pulled it up, well, it extends. The top part of it sets the pace as you pull. The harmonica extends and it keeps extending. Eventually a maximum extension is reached, and you start lifting the bottom part off the ground. I am mirroring the world in the same way. The bottom part is simply catching up by force, while the middle part is trying to hold it together. That is society today. But we need to watch out, because if the bottom part becomes too heavy … eventually the middle part breaks and there is a definite snap in society.

We all know the laws of physics. You can lift a heavy stone with a thin piece of string, as long as you pull slowly. But as soon as you pull rapidly, it snaps. How much faster can we keep pulling the harmonica until it snaps, while the bottom part is becoming increasingly heavier?

It is hard to cope in today's world, especially for someone released after serving a prison sentence, locked away for any period, whether short or long, such as Michael Fletcher. That person will find himself or herself in a new environment difficult to cope with. Education plays a crucial role in the successful reintegration of people leaving prison. The importance of education for individuals who have been incarcerated cannot be overstated. For all those who do get a second chance in life, much more can be done, as education gives access to new opportunities.

The rate of recidivism is high. Today about 3 in 4 released prisoners are rearrested because they once more did something they should not have and made a bad choice; but this may simply be because they had not been prepared for a new world. They were stranded. Recidivism among youth is even higher, with rearrests happening within the next five years.

There are a number of exemplary organizations that exist today that run special educative and vocational programs, instead of making them serve just time. Education is one of the crucial means that can help with coping—to allow a real second chance.

My interpretation of laws and legislation shall bear no reference to any judicial system of any country, nor do I wish to make any association to any systems in which prisons may be operated.

My intention here is to write a story for the reader to enjoy, but also to reflect upon.

Milton Keynes UK
Ingram Content Group UK Ltd.
UKHW030618221024
2310UKWH00026B/123